Long Shadows

With
Lee Nelson

Long
Shadows
by Wilford Meeks Halladay

This book is a work of fiction.
All of the characters in this book are fictitious
and any resemblance to actual persons,
living or dead, is purely coincidental.

Long Shadows
Published by Cedar Fort, Inc., 1991

Cedar Fort, Inc.
1182 North Industrial
Orem, UT 84057

ISBN 1-55517-72-2 Hardback edition

Distributed by

CFI
Cedar Fort, Incorporated
1182 North Industrial, Orem, UT 84057 801-226 4004

Dedicated to

Grandpa Halladay
and all his
Progeny

Acknowledgements

Sincere appreciation must be granted to my
daughter, Ann, for assisting in the typing and
helping with the miriad details of publication; to
Vilate, who encouraged me during initial writing,
and to Virginia, for additional assistance and
support;. also to Lee Nelson for invaluable input
and editing; to Lyle Mortimer and the staff at CFI
for the opportunity to tell Grandpa's story.

Long Shadows

Prologue

Early in the fall of 1990 I headed south to find and explore Robbers Roost, probably the most famous outlaw hideout in the history of the American West. I was doing research for a biographical novel on Butch Cassidy, the eighth volume in the Storm Testament series, and felt like I couldn't go any further until I had seen this legendary hideout for myself.

Derk Palfreyman of Springville, Utah, offered his guide services and six-horse trailer. We invited Mike Miller, a Houston geologist, and book publisher Lyle Mortimer to come along. Our intention was to enter and explore the roost country on horseback, the same way Cassidy and his sidekicks did a hundred years ago.

Robbers Roost is located on the southeast corner of the San Rafael desert, an area almost as remote and primitive today as it was a hundred years ago. The roost is located about half-way between Green River and Hanksville, Utah, as the crow flies, about 30 miles southeast of Goblin Valley. You won't find any houses, gas stations, fences or paved roads in this wild country, only mustangs, antelope and long horn cattle.

The cattle belong to A.C. Eckert of Hanksville, but they might as well be wild. The Roost Country provides both summer and winter range. Many of the unbranded cattle feel the sting of a rope for the first time as they are dragged, kicking and bawling, off to market. The longhorn bulls never get caught and will take after a man on horseback, if they get the notion.

The morning we rode to the Roost, the sun was blazing brightly in a cloudless Utah sky, as blue as Navajo turquoise—in elegant contrast to the orange-red sandstone bluffs. An antelope glided from hill to hill, too curious to leave, but too timid to let us get any closer.

Most writers describe the Roost country as rugged and inaccessible. Why else would generations of outlaws want to go there? This is not the case. It is a land of gentle rolling hills, marked here and there with the red sandstone bluffs mentioned already.

The outlaws came to the Roost because it was a remote place with plenty of feed for their stolen cattle and horses. Because of the scarcity of watering places, the outlaws didn't need to build fences, except for a corral for their riding horses. Their grazing herds had to return to the Roost spring every day to drink.

A few hundred yards below the spring the outlaws had a perfect escape route. The canyon comes to a narrow, abrupt end at the edge of a 20-foot cliff. Anyone wishing to continue down the canyon must lower himself over the cliff with the help of a rope. If the outlaws found themselves outgunned at the Roost, all they had to do was run down the canyon, lower themselves over the cliff, then run further down the canyon to where they kept some spare horses in a pasture. One man could easily provide cover fire as the others escaped down through the narrow chasm.

The pursuing lawmen were faced with an interesting dilemma. If they dismounted and followed the outlaws over the cliff, they would soon find themselves on foot chasing mounted riders. If, on the other hand, the officers chose to remain mounted and ride their horses around the cliffs to the pasture below, the distance was considerable, giving the outlaws too much of a head start.

It appears the outlaws never needed to use their unique escape route. According to published history only one lawman ever entered the Roost to make an arrest. He was unsuccessful and forced to return home to Green River without his horse, his boots, or his trousers.

As the red bluffs began to close in on us, we found ourselves entering a gentle canyon. Many cattle had been in the area, so we knew we were getting close to the spring. We began to see many desert holly plants, the largest I had seen, the blue-green leaves surrounded by sharp points. Some of the bushes were as high as a man on a horse, and all were covered with purple red fruit—berries about the size of small cherries. The fruit was sweet, juicy and delicious. We stopped for a minute to fill our mouths.

When we found the spring, in a gentle gully to our left, we looked to the right and saw the remains of the outlaw cabin—nothing more than a red sandstone chimney. Nearby we found what some writers had called a cave, but was nothing more than an overhang rocked up to look like a cave.

We continued down the canyon to the escape cliff already described. Using Derk's lariat, we lowered ourselves down to further check out the outlaws' escape route.

An hour later as we were returning to the spring we discovered we were not alone at the Roost. An old man, leaning against the remnants of the red chimney, was watching our approach.

There being no sign of a horse, I guessed the old-timer had walked into the Roost. I stopped to talk with him, hoping he might be able to tell me some things about the area.

"I guess this old chimney is all that's left of the outlaw cabin," I said, after saying hello to the stranger.

"I suppose their horse coral was down there," he said, pointing to the lower end of the spring. Apparently he knew the outlaws built their corral over part of the spring so the animals wouldn't have to be led to water.

The old fellow introduced himself as Wil Halladay, and before long my friends joined us as Wil continued to talk about the Roost. It soon became obvious that he knew more than was written in any of the books I had read.

I told him I thought it was strange that only one lawman had ever entered the area during outlaw occupation. I told him about the sheriff who had come to make an arrest and left without his horse, trousers or boots.

Wil disagreed with me. He said he knew of at least two other lawmen who had entered the area, conversed with Butch Cassidy, and left the area peacefully.

I asked him how he knew this. He said one of the deputy marshals to enter the Roost was Wil Halladay, his grandfather.

He said his ancestor had been a good friend of Cassidy, that they had lived and worked together in the mines at Marysvale before Cassidy had turned outlaw. The two had even courted the same woman. They had remained friends even though one was a deputy U.S. Marshal and the other a bank and train robber.

"Before I tell you any more," Wil said, "I've got to find a comfortable place to get off my feet." We found a shady spot on the north side of an old juniper tree where some flat rocks formed a rough circle. I guessed any number of horse thieves and bank robbers had sat on those same rocks, swapping stories as we were about to.

After retrieving our lunches from our saddle bags we made ourselves comfortable while Wil began to tell story after fascinating story about his grandfather, one of the first settlers in the Bryce Canyon area. Some of the stories included Butch Cassidy, who was from nearby Circleville, but many did not.

"You ought to put this material in a book," I said, after he had been talking for an hour or so.

"I have," he said.

"What's it called?" I asked.

"Just a manuscript. Hasn't been published."

Suddenly Lyle was sitting up straight on his rock. He had told me earlier he was looking for some new manuscripts to publish. There was no question but what he had a keen interest in this one, especially as the old-timer began telling us the love story between his grandfather and a woman named Laura.

It was the setting sun that finally forced us to break up our little gathering—Wil Halladay returning to his camp on the bluffs above, and the rest of us riding back to our camp.

A few weeks later Lyle showed me the Halladay manuscript. He asked me to write a prologue and help with the editing. I quickly agreed to get involved in the story that had been so fascinating as we sat on those flat rocks at Robber's Roost. The interactions with Butch Cassidy were interesting, but most of all I remember the love story between Wil and Laura. Following is that story, in the deputy's own words, as told by his grandson.

Chapter I

Love is hard to figure. You can't make it happen, and you can't make it go away. It can descend upon you with such force, filling you to the brim with so much happiness that you don't care about things like eating and sleeping. It can make you so sad you can feel things churning and tearing inside you. It can even make you angry enough to kill a man, as it did me.

Of course, I didn't know any of this when I first met Laura. I was only eighteen at the time and didn't know much of anything, except how to throw a rope and shoot a six gun.

How do you begin to tell about a woman who left a comfortable life in a beautiful home to head into an unsettled wilderness with a young man she met only a few short months earlier?

I suppose I should start at the beginning, not the real beginning, but when I first met Laura. It was in Marysvale, a little mining town in south-central Utah. The year was 1888.

I was living in a bunkhouse, converted from a chicken coop, in the backyard of an old woman named Molly Skinner. She had other live-in guests who stayed in the big house with her. Because my bunk partner and I worked in the mines and came home dusty and dirty every day, I think she liked having us in the bunk house, though we were allowed to come in the big house to share breakfast and supper with the other guests.

My bunk partner was Roy Parker, a young man from nearby Circle Valley. He was a couple of years older than I was, and seemed to know everyone in town, especially the single girls and women. Thanks to Roy I had met more new friends the last few months than I had met during the entire rest of my life before coming to Marysvale— but the most important introduction was still to come. At the upcoming dance at the town hall on Saturday night Roy had promised to introduce me to Laura Bybe.

Though Roy and I had become great friends, he still loved to tease me. It was good-natured teasing, and because I was younger than him, I let him get away with it, though I'm not sure I had any choice in the matter.

It was a couple of days before the dance that my chance to meet Laura was almost lost forever. We had just finished supper when Roy invited me to come with him down to the saloon for a game of poker with some of the boys.

"You go without me. There's still some daylight left," I responded. "I think I'll shoot a little, while I can still see."

"You aim to be a gunfighter?" he asked, his expression suddenly sober. He was probably wondering why I had to be practicing all the time when there was fun to be had.

"No, nothin' like that," I responded thoughtfully, drawing my new Colt .44 from its holster and checking the cylinder. "Just always wanted a gun like this. Couldn't afford one until now. But now that I have it I want to learn how to use it. I'd rather shoot than drink and play cards, any day."

"You like that gun, don't you?" he asked.

"I sure do," I replied.

"I like my gun too," he said as he turned toward the door. "Come on down when you get through."

I liked Roy. I had never lived with anyone outside my own family before and I was glad to have found such a good bunk mate.

I sometimes had the feeling that Roy missed his younger brothers and sisters, and was somehow using me as a replacement, someone he could protect and take care of.

I appreciated his concern for me, but I figured as soon as I had a few more weeks practice with the new Colt, I wouldn't need his protection, or anybody else's. I would be perfectly able to defend myself.

On several occasions Roy had gone up the draw to practice with me, and though I had owned the gun less than two weeks, I could already out shoot Roy. While he socialized and played poker, I practiced. Every day after work, until dark, I practiced drawing and shooting at pebbles, pieces of glass, and empty tin cans.

When I was eight my father gave me a new lariat, along with a very sober lecture on the virtues of practice. I believed what he told me and began throwing loops, thousands every month. I started on the family cow until she had been roped so much that she just ignored my loops. Then I graduated to the pigs. Learning to jerk up the slack quick enough to keep a pig in the loop required a lot of discipline.

My father promised me that one day we would go out west and get a big cattle ranch, and when we did he would need a top hand with a rope. I intended to be that top hand. It was not long before I could throw a loop with more accuracy than any grown man I knew, including my father. Now, it was my intention to become just as good with a gun as I was with a rope, and I believed lots of practice would enable me to accomplish that.

The fact that I was alone while I practiced didn't bother me. Whereas Roy always seemed to want to have people around him, I liked being alone.

I returned my Colt to its holster and walked around the big house to the street. The road that led up the canyon ran in front of the boarding house. I hustled across it and headed for the footbridge that crossed the little stream that ran through the middle of town.

Soon I reached the low hill on the north side of town and started climbing. I walked over the top and dropped into the small ravine where we did our practicing. Pieces of bottles and cans showing signs of repeated hits were strewn about.

I picked up the best pieces I could find for targets and lined them in a row against the hill. Then I began to draw and shoot. Previous experience had taught me that when I let my gun hang low I could draw quicker and with more ease. Also I learned that when I placed my left foot forward, I had better balance.

I kept popping away at the targets until it was too dark to see. Rather than return home, I headed for the saloon to join Roy.

I felt confidence and power with the new Colt on my hip as I walked toward the saloon. I followed some other men in and soon located Roy.

"Wil," he shouted and waved. "Over here."

He was at the bar with some of his friends. I walked over to him and stood by his stool.

"Thought you boys were going to play poker?" I asked.

"We've been waiting for you," Roy said. "Here, have a drink." He poured some whiskey into a glass.

"Maybe just one," I said as I picked up the drink. I didn't want to look like a tenderfoot, especially with my new Colt hanging on my hip. Roy knew I wasn't much of a drinker so he didn't put too much in the glass.

We were having a good time, and between the stories and laughing, we ended up drinking more than our empty stomachs could safely absorb. Finally Roy stood up and raised his glass. "Here's to my friend, Wil, the best shot in town," he bragged.

"How good are you?" one of the boys asked.

By that time I was so far gone that I didn't know what I was saying. I put my empty glass down, pulled out my revolver and raised it in the air.

"I can shoot that glass off the top of your head," I boasted.

"Not mine," the fellow responded as he staggered away.

"Coward," blurted Roy. "I'll do it. I'm not afraid."

He staggered toward the wall, not far away. We were both too dizzy to count our fingers or toes. When Roy reached the wall he leaned against it and placed his glass on his head. But he couldn't keep it there until he leaned his head back against the boards.

"I'm ready!" he shouted. "Open fire."

By then the men had cleared out of our way and the barkeeper had sent for the marshal. I half fell off the stool as I turned to look for Roy.

Just then the marshal came through the door. He could see at a glance that we were drunk, and that our horse play was getting too dangerous. He saw me standing there swaying back and forth waving my gun in the air, getting ready to shoot at the glass on Roy's head.

"Wil, you know better than to bring a gun in here," he said.

"I'm going to shoot a glass off Roy's head," I responded, happily.

"A little dangerous, don't you think?" he asked.

"I know what I'm doing," I boasted. "Just watch." I pointed the gun at Roy.

"Wait a minute, let me take your gun," the marshal said, stepping toward me.

"Nobody takes my gun," I challenged, a defiant tone in my voice. "Stay back. I'm not going to hurt my best friend."

"Roy might move and you could miss the glass," the marshal reasoned. "Why don't you let me have your gun until tomorrow. Then we know you won't hurt him." The marshal moved closer to me as he talked.

"Now look, Mister," I said as I turned toward him. "I'm all right. I won't hurt Roy. Now move back and leave me alone." I knew he was close to me, but I didn't realize how close. I had barely gotten the words out of my mouth when the marshal's fist hit my chin while his other hand grabbed my Colt. The last thing I remember hearing was a click.

When I awoke the next day I didn't know where I was. I strained to look around the room but my eyes burned and I couldn't see straight. I tried to sit up but my head ached terribly. I must have groaned aloud for the deputy came in to talk to me.

"How are you feeling?" he asked.

I sat up holding my head. "What happened? Where am I?"

"You're in jail," he answered. He opened the cell door and handed me a cup of coffee. He stood looking at me.

"Don't you remember the saloon and Roy with the glass on his head?" he asked.

"I think I remember a little bit," I said, the events of the previous evening beginning to come back to me. I paused for a moment as I sipped on the hot coffee.

"It seems I can remember hearing the click of a gun. I hope it wasn't mine, was it?" I asked, looking up at the deputy. The thought worried me.

"The marshal said you probably wouldn't remember anything," he answered.

"I sure hope I didn't do anything more stupid than drink on an empty stomach. What happened?"

16

He told me what the marshal had told him.

"What about the click?" I asked. "That sound seems to stick in my brain."

"Yes, there was a click. It was your gun. You shot at the marshal as he hit you with his fist."

"What happened?" I asked.

"Your gun was empty."

"Thank the Lord for that," I said, relieved.

"The marshal doesn't blame you completely," he said. "Of course, the barkeeper should never have let you in with a gun on your hip. The marshal really gave him the devil last night for letting you young bucks drink so much."

"He won't have to worry any more," I promised. "At least he won't have to worry about me." I handed him the empty cup.

"The marshal said for me to send you home when you woke up. Your gun is hanging on a peg in there by the desk. Here's your hat if you can stand to put it on. I hope you've learned your lesson."

"Thanks," I said as I staggered out of the jail cell.

Chapter II

When I arrived back at the bunk house, Roy was still snoring. I sat down on him and pinched his nose. Gasping for air, he sat up quickly, rolling me towards the foot of the bed.

"What in the devil are you trying to do?" he yelled. Then he grabbed his head. "Did someone hit me?"

"No," I answered. "But I should have, for getting me drunk last night."

"You got drunk on your own," he challenged. "What did the marshal charge you with?"

"Nothing. He said he knew it was all your fault so he let me go."

Roy didn't even look up. He knew I was only kidding him as he and the marshal were good friends. He sat on the side of the bed holding his head in his hands. I'm sure he felt as bad as I did.

That was the first and last time I ever drank like that. I guess it was a good lesson. From then on, if I ever went into a saloon, I always left after one drink or without any drink at all.

Every Saturday night was a big event in Marysvale. That's when the dances were held at the town hall. I wasn't a good dancer but I loved to try. We hadn't done much dancing back in Iowa where I was raised, and there had been no time to learn anything like that while crossing the plains with a wagon train. It seemed I was always herding cattle or out hunting food for the camp.

I loved to hunt, though. I had done it all my life. I started following my dad into the woods when I was barely big enough to walk. Father taught me how to track and how to find the places where the game would feed and hide. I learned well, so while we were coming west I was always glad when I could turn the cattle herding over to my younger brother, Ned, and the other boys, and go hunting.

I was a good shot with a rifle and a pistol. Many times as a boy I would slip into the woods and return with game for our table while my father worked the land. Mother never did like to see me go alone, but she worried less as I grew older and she was always glad to get the meat for the family. Those growing-up days seemed like a lifetime away.

My shift in the mine often went very slowly. I loved the outdoors, and continually wished I could be doing something outside. I missed my family, and had it not been for Roy's good-natured company I would have missed my family a lot more.

One thing I knew for sure. I would not stay in the mines very long, just long enough to earn some money to buy more livestock while Father kept looking for a place to start the big cattle ranch we wanted so badly. In the meantime I would continue to sharpen my roping and shooting skills while killing boredom by attending the Saturday night dances.

"Why did you come clear out here to this wild country?" Roy asked one Saturday night as we were getting ready for the dance.

"Dad didn't want to be a farmer," I responded. "He always talked about owning a large cattle ranch and we just decided to come west and start one."

"Have you found the place you want, yet?" he asked.

"I don't know. We started traveling south when we reached Salt Lake. When we got here I told Dad I'd work in the mines and earn some extra money to buy livestock while he looked for that ranch. They went up the Sevier River looking for land while I worked. My brother, Ned, will come for me when they get located."

Roy told me his family had settled on a farm in Circle Valley to the south a few years earlier. Roy said he was like my father and didn't want to be a farmer either, so he came to the mines. I asked him how long he thought he would stay.

"I'm not sure," he said. "I think I'll try the mines in Colorado some day. But tell me about the plains states. Wasn't there plenty of land there for a cattle ranch?"

I told him there were millions of acres of rolling prairies, but Dad didn't want that. He wanted to locate near the mountains where there would be trees, fishing, and hunting.

I told him about coming west and the many opportunities I had to hunt for the wagon train. I even told him about a run-in I had with some Indians.

Roy told me about an Indian who worked at the mine. He was a chief and was earning money to buy food for his tribe. His name was Charley. I had noticed Charley before, but didn't know he was an Indian.

I told him about a young Indian named Red Owl I had met on the way west. I told him Red Owl had saved my life. Roy was eager to hear all about it.

"All right," I said. "I'll tell you about Red Owl tomorrow if tonight you'll introduce me to those girls who sing with the band."

"You mean the Bybe girls?" he asked.

"Yes, I'd like to meet the older one. I believe her name is Laura."

"Come on then," Roy said as he started for the door. We walked out of the bunk house and down the road toward the dance hall which was located in the center of town.

The dance had already started when we arrived. We went in and stood next to the wood burning stove for a few minutes. It was a chilly fall evening and the fire felt good.

Soon Roy was dancing, but not before he introduced me to several young ladies. It wasn't long until I was dancing too. It was a challenge for them to teach me, but they were good sports and kept trying.

After a while the Bybe girls came in. I think I was the first to notice. Tonight Roy would introduce me to Laura. Though I had seen her on several previous occasions, she had never looked more beautiful. My palms began to sweat.

Then I could feel the hair on the back of my neck stand on end as I saw who followed Laura and her sister through the door. It was Harry Dawson, one of the boys who worked in the mines.

I didn't like Harry, and Roy didn't either. He was a handsome young man with black, curly hair and large, striking eyes. At work, he always seemed to end up with the easiest jobs. He didn't like hard work, and didn't mind not doing his share. It was as if he had always been able to get by on good looks and a smooth tongue, and was determined to continue doing that as long as he could.

22

What I disliked most about Harry was the way he talked about women. Though he wasn't any older than me, he bragged about all the women he had slept with. Frequently, to the men at the mine, he would brag about vulgar things he did with women when he got them alone at night. I figured he was lying, or certainly grossly exaggerating, and wondered why he would do that.

As I looked over at the door it appeared Harry said something to tease Laura. She responded by laughing, placing her hand on his arm, and playfully pushing him away.

For the first time in my life I knew what it was like to feel jealous—and I hadn't even met the woman. I wanted to run over and protect her from that smooth-talking low life. I felt angry and confused.

The next thing I knew Harry asked Laura to dance, and she accepted. I found myself wishing my gun was on my hip so I could kill him, though I knew I wouldn't really do such a thing.

After a few more dances, Laura and her sister walked up to the stage to sing. They stood near the front of the stage just in front of the piano. Although the lights were poor I could see Laura's unmistakable smile. Her sister was beautiful too, but Laura was absolutely the most beautiful woman I had ever seen or ever hoped to see. Her wide blue eyes and sorrel hair caused a strange throbbing in my chest.

I had grown up on the frontier and while traveling west and working in the mines, the chance to see a pretty girl didn't come very often. Still, I felt myself a pretty good judge of female beauty, and I had just discovered the mother lode.

No one danced while the Bybe girls sang. Everyone gathered around the piano and listened. The girls sang beautifully together. Everyone was hungry to hear good music.

We gave them a rousing hand when they finished. I couldn't keep my eyes off Laura as she walked off the stage. Roy met Laura at the bottom of the stairs and brought her straight toward me while the band started playing a song for the next dance.

I stood paralyzed as Roy and Laura came nearer.

"Steady old boy," I said to myself. "You asked for this."

"Wil," Roy said, as they walked up to me. "I've told Laura about you and she's agreed to teach you how to dance. This is my bunk partner, Wil Halladay," he said to Laura.

"Hello, Wil," she said, smiling at me. "Roy has told me a lot about you. I feel like I already know you."

I stood speechless. I couldn't think of anything to say, and even if I could, I wasn't sure I would have been able to get it out.

"Go on, Wil," Roy said. "Don't be afraid. She won't bite you. She's a good dancer and will help you learn all the steps."

I can't even remember what I mumbled as she took hold of my sweaty hand and led me onto the dance floor. My timidity seemed to give her confidence.

"Don't be afraid," she said, softly. "I've watched you dance before and you learn fast. It won't take you long to learn all I know." She smiled.

She showed me a few steps of the dance and then she suggested we follow another couple. We slipped in behind an older man and woman who were dancing smoothly. I watched carefully and Laura helped when she could. Soon the steps began to fall into place and I think Laura could see the joy in my face.

By the time the dance came to an end I had relaxed a little and was more sure of myself. I didn't want her to leave me to dance with anyone else, so I just stood where we had stopped and told her how much I enjoyed her singing.

"That's the main reason I come to the dances," I said, amazed that I was being so bold so soon.

"Thank you," she said. "But you like to dance too, don't you?"

"Oh, yes, I really do," I admitted. "Especially with you."

She blushed a little at my remark. I was glad I had been so bold. The music began and we started a new dance. It was one I knew something about so Laura didn't have to help me very much.

When that dance ended I still didn't want to let her go, but I was afraid my affection for her was too conspicuous and my desire to stay with her might cause her some embarrassment. I walked her over to where her sister, Leah and Harry were standing, thanked her for the dancing lessons, then wandered over to the big stove.

I had never felt like this before and it really bothered me. My emotions were all mixed up. I wasn't sure I understood what was happening.

When I looked back to see what Laura was doing, she was dancing with Harry. I wanted to hurry over and jerk her away from him. I wanted to punch Harry in the face and break all his beautiful teeth. I wanted to take Laura away with me, I knew not where.

This was all too confusing. I turned and headed out the door.

I walked back to the bunk house trying to figure things out. I had never liked a girl before so this was a new experience for me. To see her dance caused me pain. I decided it had to be love, but it was sure different than what I thought love would be like.

I was still awake trying to figure it all out when Roy came in. "What happened?" he asked. "You disappeared like a ghost. Weren't you having a good time?"

26

"Oh, yes. But I have a problem and I figured I'd come home and think about it."

"Want to talk about it?"

"Maybe tomorrow," I answered.

I think Roy started snoring before he pulled the covers over his chest. I listened to him for a long time before I finally dozed off.

Chapter III

The next day was Sunday so we both slept in. Roy's snoring finally woke me so I woke him.

"What's up?" he asked as my pillow hit him in the face.

"You won't let me sleep so I'm not going to let you sleep," I told him.

"But today's Sunday," he groaned. "Go back to sleep." He turned his face to the wall and pulled the pillow over his head.

I couldn't go back to sleep, but I figured Roy was entitled to stay in bed as long as he wanted. I had plenty to think about anyway.

As I lay there my thoughts of Laura picked up where they left off the night before. I wondered if I got up and went to church, if I might be able to analyze my feelings better. I crawled out of bed, dressed quietly and walked out into the crisp air. I remembered the town's only church, a Mormon chapel, was near the dance hall.

Lost in my thoughts, I walked down the road, breathing deeply the fresh morning air. I was almost to the church before I noticed others hurrying to the building. Slowly, I walked up the steps and quietly slipped into an empty spot on one of the rear benches.

It seemed good to be in church again. I went often with my family when I was growing up, but traveling across the country hadn't provided us much of a chance to attend any meetings. I usually felt comfortable and peaceful in church.

Looking around, I noticed a few people I had seen before but no one I wanted to speak to.

A man stood up to start the meeting. I watched him closely and listened carefully as he announced an opening song. I looked over at the organ. There sat Laura, ready to play.

She was looking straight at me. When I looked at her, she smiled. My heart began to pound. I decided I must be in love.

I wondered what I should do. I couldn't let her know. Her father was a big shot lawyer and Laura was one of the most popular girls for miles around. I didn't own anything but a job in a mine. I didn't even own a team and wagon. What was I thinking? She was probably smiling at me, not because she liked me but because she thought it strange to see the likes of me in church.

When the song started I stood up with the rest of the congregation, but I didn't try to sing. I was too deep in thought. When the bishop finally got up to speak, he gave a long sermon. I don't think I heard a word he said, for while he was talking, I kept trying to steal a side glance at Laura. When she wasn't looking at me I was looking at her.

My heart and mind were taking turns arguing with each other. One second my mind would say "run" but the next second my heart would say "stay." Such was my confusion.

At the end of the meeting everyone but me stood up and moved slowly toward the front door. I stayed where I was, still confused, but enjoying that feeling of comfort I usually felt in church.

I was sitting there with my head down, trying to sort out my feelings and thoughts when someone walked up to me. I turned my head and looked up to see Laura's smiling eyes.

"Hello," she said.

"Hello," I said as I jumped up. Unconsciously, I think I lingered behind hoping something like this might happen. As I gazed at her, overwhelmed by her beauty, there was a weakness in my knees that made me think that perhaps I should sit back down again.

"I'm glad to see you here," Laura said.

"I've always liked going to church," I replied, hoping she would believe I was sincere.

"That's good."

"May I walk you home?" I asked. "Or are you with someone else?" I hadn't noticed Harry Dawson in the meeting.

"I'm alone today," she said. "I'd be happy to have your company."

We walked to the door and down the wooden steps. The sun was shining brightly but the air was cool.

"What happened last night?" she asked. "You left so suddenly. Did I say or do something wrong?"

"Oh, no," I replied quickly. I didn't want to tell her how much it had bothered me to see her talking and dancing with Harry Dawson. "I just had a problem I was trying to solve," I added.

"Did you get it solved?" she asked.

"No, I'm still working on it," I replied.

We walked in silence for a few minutes. Finally Laura spoke. "May I ask you a question, Wil?"

"Sure, anything," I said without thinking. "Ask anything you want."

"I hope I'm not being too forward," she said, "But are you alone, or do you have a family?"

"I have a wonderful family! I have a father and mother, a younger brother, Ned, and two sisters, Nancy and Ellen."

"Where are they? Do they live close by?"

"It's a long story," I answered.

"I have lots of time," she smiled.

I told her how I had grown up near the Mississippi River. It was a beautiful place but father didn't want to be a farmer. He'd always wanted to be a cattle rancher so we decided to move west.

I told her how we originally decided to go to Oregon. But Dad wanted to see the Great Basin first, so we headed south once we entered the Utah Territory. When we reached Marysvale I decided I'd work in the mines to earn some money to buy more livestock. My father and the rest of the family continued their journey up the Sevier River, looking for possible places to start the cattle ranch.

I told her how my brother, Ned, had rode into town a few weeks earlier to tell me they were going to wait until spring before moving any further south. He said Dad was exploring the valleys to the south and east.

"Do you think he has found what he wants?" she asked.

"I don't know about him, but I have." I gasped at what I had said without thinking.

"You mean you like the mines?" she asked, somewhat surprised, missing what I had really meant in my careless comment.

"The mines give me quick cash," I answered, hoping to keep her distracted from my original comment.

When we reached the front gate to her father's big house it was too chilly to stand there very long. I turned and looked at her.

"Will you do me a favor?" I asked.

"Sure," she replied. "What is it?"

"Will you go to the dance with me next Saturday night?" I was amazed at my boldness, and a little proud too.

She smiled as she looked up into my eyes. "I'd be happy to go with you, Wil," she answered.

I was so happy I didn't know what else to say. I looked at her and mumbled a thank you. I knew I had to get away or I would probably make a fool of myself. I mumbled something else as I turned and started for home. I can't remember what it was I said.

Without stopping I ran down the street, around the corner and up to the bunk house. When I reached the door I was so out of breath I had to sit down on the steps for a minute. While sitting there I let my dreams run wild. I had a date with the prettiest girl in town. I didn't know much about dancing but that hadn't seemed to make any difference to her, nor the fact that she knew very little about me. I was surprised at the events of the day.

I decided it was because I was a friend of Roy's that she agreed to go to the dance with me. Roy knew everybody and everyone liked him. Maybe Roy brought good luck to those around him. He did for me.

Before we got very far into winter that year, I had learned all the dance steps and had come a long way in overcoming my bashfulness. Roy said he believed it was because of my association with

Laura, and Laura said she believed it was because of my association with Roy.

I worked hard in the mines that winter and escorted Laura to all the dances, and to church. I didn't start out with the intent of going to church every week, but with Laura there I didn't mind at all.

Chapter IV

Late one March afternoon Ned rode into town. He tied Pete—the old gelding we brought all the way from Iowa—to a tree and went into the boarding house to inquire about me. The landlady told him I would be home about sun down and that he could wait for me in the front room. Later he told me how good it felt to sit in a house again where it was warm.

At our usual time Roy and I came walking down the road from work.

"Hey, there's Pete," I yelled.

"Who's Pete?" Roy asked.

"My little horse," I answered, "the one I rode all the way from Iowa. The one I loaned to my little brother when I came to work at the mine." I hurried to Pete and patted him on the nose and neck. I was sure he recognized me too. "You look a little thin old boy," I said. I figured Ned was nearby. I hoped he wasn't bringing bad news.

As I walked into the house, Ned rose to greet me. He was thin and sun-tanned. He looked real good.

"Hello, little brother," I said. Ned grabbed hold of me and I was so glad to see him.

"Is everyone all right?" I asked. He nodded in the affirmative. "Ned, meet my bunk partner, Roy Parker," I added. They shook hands and Roy excused himself and headed out back to the bunk house.

"We're well," Ned began. "But it's been cold. Father and I dug a cave in the hillside and fixed it up the best we could, with the tent in front, but I never seem to get warm. This house feels too good to be true."

"How did the stock come through the winter?" I asked.

"They're thin but still on their feet. We haven't even had to slaughter one this winter." He said he kept the family in meat with rabbits and deer. The sagebrush flats and foothills had lots of rabbits and coyotes. The coyote pelts made good rugs on the floor of the tent."

"Has Father found a place yet?" I asked.

"That's what I came in to tell you. Dad thinks he's found a spot to start our ranch."

"Where?" I asked.

"South and east about 60 or 70 miles. He says it's down below some breaks where it's warm and where there is lots of open country for winter grazing."

"What's the plan?"

"He wants to start moving as soon as the snow melts and the wagon won't mire in the mud. He says we'll head up the west fork of the river to where it opens into Panguitch Valley. The meadows are good there and we can stay until the cattle fill up before moving on."

Ned explained that from there we would go southeast through a red canyon and on over a sagebrush plateau to the breaks. He said the road was new and rough.

"Dad wants you to come when you can," Ned concluded. "Or have you decided to stay here?"

"No, Ned," I said. "I've been underground long enough. I'd rather have the sun, moon and stars. I want to buy a new saddle horse when I leave. Tell Dad to wait for me in the Panguitch Meadows. I'll meet you there."

I told him about the tall young horse I planned to buy and said he could have Pete as his very own now.

When Ned said it was time to start heading back, I urged him to stay with us for the night. I asked Mrs. Skinner if he could eat with us, then sleep in the bunkhouse with Roy and me. She said it was all right. We took Pete down to the livery stable.

I knew Ned would like to sleep in a bed again. Besides, I didn't want him to ride back up along the river after dark. The ground would be frozen and the night cold.

Ned told me about the river that forked some fifteen miles upstream. One stream went southeast and the other ran mostly in a southerly direction. He told me not to follow the river when I left, but to go straight south over the sagebrush flats. He said I could pick up the trail when I reached Circle Valley.

Over dinner Ned and Roy talked about Circle Valley and the surrounding area. Roy knew all the places Ned mentioned. He even knew about the place where Dad wanted to settle. He had chased cattle down that way.

"It's a good place for cattle," Roy said. "You could take them down below the breaks in the fall and drive them back up on the mountain for the summer. There's good feed along the east fork of the Sevier in the summer. The only problem is the distance from other towns, and the road down over the breaks is almost impassible in bad weather. But it's a good place to raise cattle. The lower country runs for miles and miles, clear to the Colorado River," he added.

"Dad wanted that kind of a place so I guess he'll be happy," Ned said.

We spent the rest of the evening talking about Mother and Dad and the girls. I didn't know how or what to tell Ned about Laura, but I did tell him that she had taught me how to dance and that I had been going to church with her. I was sure that would please Mother.

The next morning Ned left when we started for the mine. I hated to see him go. We had been close pals all our lives and seeing him again made me realize how much I had missed his company, but I knew I would be back with him soon.

Chapter V

I continued to court Laura, though I didn't tell her about Ned's visit and my plans to leave. Often I would walk over to her place in the evenings after work while Roy went to the saloon. I knew I was deeply in love with her and wondered how I was going to be able to leave without her. I wasn't going to spend my life in the mines. I wanted to be out in the open and to be with my family. Father hoped Ned and I would be partners with him in his cattle adventure and that was all right with me.

What was I going to do about Laura? That question bothered me day and night. I sure didn't want to leave her, but I didn't have the courage to ask her to marry me, but there was no other way for us to remain together.

I didn't know how she felt about me. I figured she must like me a lot or she wouldn't have been so nice, and wouldn't have gone to the dances and church with me every week. What was I going to do?

One night in late April, as we were walking home after the regular Saturday night dance, Laura stopped me from opening her front gate. I looked at her in the bright moonlight, wondering what she was doing. Her eyes were sober and her usual smile was gone.

"What's wrong, Wil?" she asked. "You have been very quiet all evening."

I looked at her without saying a word. She gazed up at me, waiting. I just didn't know how to say it.

"Well," I began, "I have a problem and I don't know how to solve it."

"Is there trouble at the mine?" she asked.

"No," I answered.

"Is it something I can help you with?" she asked.

"Yes, I think you could."

"Then please tell me," she begged.

"It's like this. Father found the place he wants and I want to go with them. I plan to quit the mine next week and head up the river to join them"

Laura just stood there, looking up at me. She didn't say anything. I looked into her beautiful face.

"You see, Laura," I began with hesitation, almost a stutter. "I don't want to go alone. I love you. Won't you please come with me?"

My heart was pounding and my hands were cold and clammy.

She looked into my eyes and smiled.

"Is this a proposal?"

"I guess it is," I answered. "I love you so much. I don't want to lose you. Maybe you don't love me as much as I love you but don't you think you could in time? Please say yes," I pleaded.

"You don't know how I've waited to hear you say you love me," she said as she put her arms around me and held me tight. "Now you can't get away without me."

As her words gradually began to sink into my brain, I hugged her so tight she could hardly breathe. It was hard to believe this was happening to me.

"You mean you'll marry me?" I asked.

"I will, any day," she said with a big grin.

I kissed her and swung her around and around. I think I was the happiest young man on earth. Suddenly a thought hit me like a bolt of lightening.

"What about your parents? Will they let you?"

"I think they will," she responded. "They want me to be happy, and marrying you will do that."

"But I have so little to offer you," I said. "I don't have a home to take you to. They might object to that."

"We'll build one together," she said. "We'll go with your parents and settle in the new place. We'll grow food, raise crops and have lots of cattle. I love you, Wil, and I want to be with you."

42

I was so excited I had a hard time thinking straight, but I didn't care right then.

"I'd better go in now, Wil," Laura said. "There'll be so much to do before the wedding. I'm not sure I can get everything ready in time. Can we wait two weeks to leave?"

"Sure," I said. "I haven't said anything to anyone but you. We'll plan to leave in two weeks then."

"Thank you, Wil. I must go in and tell Mother now so we can get started."

"If you tell her tonight, maybe no one will get any sleep," I said, as we walked up on the porch. I hugged her again, and kissed her goodnight. "You've just made me the happiest person in the world. Goodnight. I love you so very much."

"I'll tell you what," she said, looking up at me. "You pick me up for church in the morning. Come home with me afterwards and eat Sunday dinner with us. We'll tell them the good news then. Tomorrow afternoon Mother and I can start making plans."

I agreed to go along with her plan, but told her I couldn't stay long, because I had to start looking for a team and wagon. I couldn't take her away on the back of my saddle horse.

"Daddy will help you find an outfit," she said.

For the third time that evening I gave her a big hug and kiss. Then I headed for the boarding house. I looked up at the bright sky, took a deep breath and shouted to the moon, telling it how happy I was.

Then I hurried to my room. Roy's breathing was deep and regular. He was asleep. I sat down on the side of his bed and took hold of his nose. His mouth opened and he gasped. He half sat up and saw me in the moonlight.

"Are you trying to smother me again?" he grumbled.

"No, I just wanted to tell you the latest news," I said.

"Can't it wait 'till morning?" he asked. "I'm sleepy."

"I'm not," I informed him.

"Well it must be something big. Out with it," he said, propping his head up on his folded pillow.

"I'm going to quit the mine and leave," I said casually.

He looked at me, a puzzled expression on his face. "I don't blame you, but is that what you woke me up for? I'm going back to sleep."

"There's more news. Laura has agreed to go with me," I blurted out. A big smile spread across his face. He reached over and grabbed my hand.

"Don't you think you should ask her to marry you first?" he asked.

"I did and she said yes."

"When's the big day?"

"About two weeks. Won't be long."

"I think that's great. Laura's a wonderful girl. I hope both of you will be very happy. I wish I was ready to settle down like you, but I'm just too restless. Maybe I'll quit the mine when you leave and try something else. I'm getting tired of this work, anyway."

Roy settled back in bed and was soon asleep. I didn't go to sleep for hours. When I awoke I had to hurry to meet Laura in time for church. She was waiting for me and we hurried down the road.

The church service that day was all a blur. I couldn't keep my mind on anything but Laura. Finally it was over and we headed up the street toward her home.

As we ate dinner I kept waiting for Laura to make the announcement. I'd look at her and she'd smile. I didn't know how she could keep our secret this long. Finally she put her fork down and cleared her throat. Mr. and Mrs. Bybe looked at her and so did Leah.

"Daddy, Mother," Laura began, with some hesitation. "Last night Wil asked me to marry him, and I told him I would."

Mrs. Bybe gasped. Mr. Bybe looked at Laura and then at me. "Laura are you sure you want to do this?" he asked.

"Yes, Daddy, I do."

"Have you made any plans?" he asked, looking straight at me. I could tell he really wanted me to answer that question.

"Well," I said, squirming under his gaze. "I plan to stay with the mine until the end of next week. By then I should have enough money saved to buy a team and wagon, a saddle horse and a few more cattle. After the wedding, we'll travel up the river till we catch up with my family. Father has found the place where he wants to settle. I'd like to leave two weeks from tomorrow, if we can. I want to be part of our cattle operation and I can't do it here in the mines."

"Laura, do you think you can be happy on a ranch?" he asked.

"I think I can be happy any place with Wil," she answered.

"Then I think it's settled," he said. "You and your mother make the arrangements for the wedding. I hope you've thought it through seriously and that you'll be happy." As he stood up to leave he squeezed Laura's hand and smiled at her.

"Thank you, Daddy," she said as she stood to give him a hug. "I love you very much."

He turned to me and reached out his hand. "My boy, I hope you will take good care of my little girl."

"I surely will," I promised. "Do you know of anyone who wants to sell a team and wagon?"

"Not offhand," he answered. "But I'll ask around. We ought to be able to find one all right."

Chapter VI

Before we finished eating, Laura, her Mother and Leah began to make wedding preparations. I felt like I was in the way, so I told Laura I was going to find Roy.

Getting ready for the wedding took so much of Laura's time that I only saw her a short while each evening. Roy and I started looking for a team and wagon. We asked the men in the saloon if they knew of anything for sale. We didn't hear of anything encouraging, but one day in the mine one of the workers said he had a wagon and team that he might sell. He had moved to the area during the winter looking for a farm. Not being able to locate one at the time, he decided to work in the mines until spring. He had brought two wagons and teams with him to the mine and he was willing to sell one of them.

After work that night, Roy and I went to look at the outfit. The horses looked good and the wagon had new bows and a wagon cover on it. The rest looked sturdy and in good condition. It was just what I wanted, so the next day I gave the man a down payment on it.

"Are you still going to buy a saddle horse?" Roy asked.

"Yes," I answered. "I gave my old horse to Ned."

"Bybe has some nice horses."

"Especially the big sorrel behind the house. But I'm afraid if I asked him to sell me one he'd want to give it to me. I'd love to have the big sorrel, but I don't want to impose on him. Anyway, I think he wants to keep that horse for himself."

"Do you have another horse in mind?"

"I think I'll go to the livery stable and put $10.00 down on the black colt—the tall one. Dan said he is green broke."

That evening after work we walked down to the livery stable to look at the horse. I paid Dan a $10.00 down payment. I told him I would pick up the horse and give him the rest of the money just before I left town. Dan said that was all right with him.

As word of the wedding spread around the town the excitement grew. The manager of the dance hall went to Laura and her Mother and offered the hall for the wedding. He felt the community owed Laura a favor for singing so many times for them, free. He said they would arrange for the bishop to be there at 9:30 P.M. to marry us. He volunteered to do all the advertising and help with the refreshments.

As there were only about ten days left and so much to do, Mrs. Bybe agreed. Laura said she and Leah would sing some extra songs that night.

A few days later Roy and I bought some tools and grease for the wagon. We wanted to get it ready for the journey before we picked it up. A few days later I paid the rest of the money on the team and wagon and moved them up to Laura's so we could load it when we wanted. Mr. Bybe said I could leave the team in the barn until we left.

It bothered me that Harry Dawson continued to hang around. He was lazy and when he drank he was a pain in the neck, which was most of the time. What I suppose bothered me most was the fact that the women couldn't seem to see beyond his good looks and suave way. He thought he was a Romeo and the girls seemed to swoon when he came around. Even Mrs. Bybe beamed when he praised her. He was smooth like a snake. Most of the time he chased Leah but she was not his only lady friend. I didn't like him and I think Mr. Bybe felt about the same toward him as I did.

For a while Harry and I worked on the same shift at the mine, but he spent so much time sitting around rolling his Bull Durhams that he eventually lost his job. Now, he would go from one mine to another, always starting over, but never staying in one place very long.

Harry kept trying to be my friend, and I kept avoiding him. I guess he wanted to be the best man at the wedding, but I would have none of that.

During those last two weeks I saw more of Laura at church than any place. She and her Mother and sister seemed to have a million things to do to get ready. I was glad for Roy's company. He seemed to understand my nervousness and had a calming influence on me.

One night, not long before our marriage, Roy agreed to help me fix a water barrel on the wagon. But first he asked me to keep an old promise I'd made to him many months before.

"What promise is that?" I asked.

"You said you'd tell me about your Indian friend, Hoot Owl, or something like that."

"His name isn't Hoot Owl. It's Red Owl."

"Tell me about him."

"Have you known many Indians, Roy?" I asked.

"A few—mainly Charley. If they were all like him, we wouldn't have much trouble."

"Red Owl was like Charley," I said. "I hope some day I'll meet him again so I can thank him for what he did for me."

"Thank him for what?" Roy asked.

"We were traveling along the North Platte River with the rest of the wagon train one day," I began, "when I decided to ride up a ridge to see if I could locate any game. I looked to the north and out there on the open range were about a dozen buffalo. I thought of going after them, but I figured I'd better let Dad and Mother know where I had gone. I rode back to the wagon to tell them. They told me not to go too far away from the main trail alone and that if I shot anything, to come back for help. They wanted me to take someone with me but I knew I could do better alone.

I rode Pete up the ridge toward the buffalo. They were still there. I rode around the hills until I was above them, then moved carefully towards them until I was on the same ridge as they were.

I started towards them. I loaded my rifle and held it across the pommel of my saddle. The nearer I got to them, the more I leaned to the opposite side of my horse. When I was even with them I said whoa to old Pete. He stopped. I took aim at a big bull and squeezed the trigger. He dropped in his tracks. The rest of the herd stampeded up the ridge, disappearing over the top.

I suppose I should have headed for the wagons for help, but it was late. I thought I should at least clean the animal first.

Slipping my rifle back in its scabbard, I grabbed my knife and started on the buffalo. I worked fast and only looked up when I heard Pete snort. Six Indians were coming down the ridge. The one who later introduced himself as Red Owl was in the lead.

They were already very close. My rifle was out of reach, over by the horse. I feared a move toward it might bring a shot from one or more of them.

I stood and looked at them as they rode closer. I guess they were wondering if I was friendly. Finally, I raised my arms and waved for them to come close. Red Owl rode cautiously up to me. I smiled at him and told him to help himself to the meat.

I think he thought I might be pulling a trick on him, because he was careful in his approach. All the time one of the other Indians had his rifle pointed straight at me. I worried that he might pull the trigger if I made a bad move, so I smiled at Red Owl and told him my name was Wil Halladay and that I wanted to be friends. I hoped he understood me. All I had was my knife to defend me against the six Indians.

"Me Red Owl," he replied. Boy, was that music to my ears when he spoke. I held out my hand and he shook it.

"Food for all," I said, pointing at the buffalo.

Red Owl called to his companions. They dismounted, finished cleaning and skinning the animal, then cut it into quarters.

"We take one leg. You take rest," he said.

One of the Indians produced a dirty old sack. They put one of the front quarters into it. Another Indian untied my sacks from my saddle and put a hind quarter in each one before hanging them over

Pete's saddle. A second Indian helped him lift the bags. The other front quarter he tied in my rain slicker behind my saddle. I sensed they wanted the hide, so I told them to take it. One of them threw it upon his pony and started up the hill.

"Thanks, Red Owl," I said. "I hope we meet again."

"Maybe we will," he said as he jumped on his horse. He waved as he followed the others up the ridge.

I was relieved when they left and yet I felt I had gained a friend. I picked up the bridle reins and started leading Pete toward the trail.

When I topped the last ridge and started down toward the wagons it was almost dark. Dad saw me and met me halfway up the hill. When he saw I had buffalo meat in my sacks he started running towards me. I told him about my hunt and what had happened. He told me he was proud of me for making friends instead of enemies. That was always his philosophy, but he said he wished I wouldn't stay out so late anymore, especially when I was alone.

"You know, Wil," Roy said, I'd love to have adventures like that."

I think Roy meant what he said. He always seemed as if something was missing. I knew he was restless and I knew he loved excitement. Some nights when we returned from the mine he would sit down and ask endless questions about the country I came from. He wanted to know all about the fishing and hunting and the people, especially the Indians, whether they were friendly or not. I got the feeling that he would have had the time of his life coming west with a wagon train.

Chapter VII

During that same conversation Roy asked me if I had ever seen Red Owl again.

I said I had, about a week later. We were getting up to where the Sweetwater branches to the west, where we would have to cross the North Platte River and head towards the South Pass. I had left the younger boys with the cattle and was out checking for game again.

I saw some fresh deer tracks leading up a small stream to the north. I knew it was probably too late to start after it, but I figured if the deer wasn't too far ahead, I might be able to get some fresh meat for the evening meal.

"I followed the tracks along the stream until I jumped the deer. It ran into a clump of trees ahead of me before I could get a shot. Cautiously I followed.

It was after sundown when I noticed Pete prick up his ears and smell the breeze. I was flat against the horse's neck, hoping Pete would walk close to the deer without startling it. We were close when the deer snorted and started to move.

I saw him in the shadows and shot as quickly as I could. The buck staggered, then picked up speed. I rode over to where he had been standing. There was blood on the bushes so I knew he was wounded. I hurried along his trail as the light began to fade. I urged my horse into a trot trying to follow the signs and watch where I was going.

I wasn't watching carefully enough and ran into a low tree limb, hitting my head so hard it knocked me off my horse. I fell to the ground unconscious. As I fell the bridle reins dropped to the ground and Pete stopped. Luckily he stayed close by.

At the same time Red Owl and his band were across the little stream, on the opposite ridge. When they heard the shot they came to investigate. As they sat there looking around they located the wounded deer and saw Pete move. I think Red Owl had a suspicion that something was wrong or that I was stalking the deer. They waited and when nothing happened they rode down to investigate.

The deer was wounded and couldn't travel so one of Red Owl's companions put him out of his misery and proceeded to dress him out. Red Owl rode over to where Pete was standing, and saw me unconscious on the ground.

When I came to, Red Owl was wiping my face with my wet bandanna. He laid it across my forehead where a lump was beginning to swell.

I looked up, my vision foggy. I could see an Indian leaning over me, and hoped it was Red Owl.

"Oh, my head," I moaned.

"You big head." I heard him say.

I reached up and felt the lump where the pain was.

"What happened?" I asked.

"Tree," Red Owl said.

While Red Owl watched over me, his friends removed the sacks from the back of my saddle and put most of the deer meat in them. Placing an equal portion of meat in each sack, they secured the two bags together then laid them across the back of my saddle.

I tried to get up but staggered and almost fell. Red Owl grabbed me and helped me get on my horse. He guided my feet in the stirrups. I took hold of the saddle horn. My head was still going round and round.

Red Owl said something to his companions and motioned down the canyon. He jumped up on his horse, then picked up Pete's bridle reins and started leading us down the canyon.

It was dark when we reached the main trail and I was having a hard time hanging on. Red Owl watched me carefully all the way. He also kept a close eye on the wagon tracks.

Without Red Owl I never would have reached camp that night.

It was way after dark when I caught a blurry glimpse of a campfire ahead. I was doing all I could to hang on.

I remember when Pete stopped. Father pulled me off the saddle. I think I was more glad to see my parents than they were to see me.

In the excitement Red Owl disappeared like a ghost. No one saw him leave. I never saw him again. I keep hoping our paths will cross again so I can thank him. He probably saved my life.

I was half out of my mind for days. I rode in the wagon on the bedding while Mother bathed my forehead and face with cold towels and water. We were almost to the South Pass before I woke up one morning, finally able to see the mountains.

"Nothing like that has ever happened to me," Roy said. "In fact, all that has ever happened to me is work and more work. Someday I'm going to do something that has more excitement to it."

"I hope I never bump my head like that again," I said as I rubbed my head. "Now that I have told you about Red Owl," I continued, "tell me you'll be the best man at my wedding."

"Yes," Roy smiled. "I'll be there to hold you up. There is one favor you can do for me, though."

"Name it," I said.

"Here's fifty dollars I wish you'd give to Mother when you stop in Circle Valley."

"All right," I promised. I asked where in the valley I could find his family.

"Go clear through to the mouth of the canyon," he explained. "Just before you enter the canyon you'll see a log cabin sitting on the west edge of the fields. Trees are growing around the house. The corrals and yards are nearby. You can't miss it, and please be sure to tell Mother that I'm well."

I tucked the $50 deep into my pocket.

I worked until the next Friday night. I figured I'd need all day Saturday to help Laura and Mrs. Bybe finish the wedding preparations.

Saturday evening Laura and I went to the dance about nine o'clock. I think everyone in town was there. The stage and hall were decorated and the orchestra was playing when we arrived.

Laura and I started dancing but we never got halfway around the room before someone cut in. I got the feeling the whole night was going to be that way.

At 9:30 the bishop walked in and everyone who could find a seat sat down. Mrs. Bybe and Leah followed the bishop up on the stage. They motioned for me to follow. Leah was carrying Laura's veil over her arm. I left Laura standing beside her father and started for the stage with Roy. I was glad Harry kept his distance. Once in a while he used a little sense.

Roy acted as if he were holding me up as we walked across that long empty dance floor. I was nervous and thankful he was there.

We lined up and the band started playing "Here Comes the Bride." When I saw Laura and her father walking towards us, my heart almost stopped. She looked so beautiful as she smiled at me. I knew I loved her as much as any man ever loved a woman. Leah placed the veil on Laura's head as she stepped up on the stage. Laura looked at me and smiled. She reached for me. I took her hand in mine and sucked in a big breath. I knew I was shaking and I'm sure she recognized my state of shock. She squeezed my hand and then my arm. I believe she did that because she thought I might collapse.

With Laura on one side holding my arm and Roy on the other side, grinning from ear to ear, I began to feel as if I might make it. Roy punched me in the ribs and whispered in my ear, "Hang in there, Buddy, I'm sure you'll live through it." He always seemed to have the ability to meet any situation with confidence and a smile. I often wondered if he ever worried about anything.

The bishop stepped in front of us. We looked at him. A hush fell over the hall as the bishop smiled at us and began to speak.

The wedding vows were repeated and soon I was waltzing Laura around the room, basking in her beautiful smile. Others soon joined in and it was a milling, jovial group that finished the dance.

The manager stepped to the front of the stage and asked for silence. "Ladies and gentlemen," he said, "the Bybe girls have promised us some extra songs tonight as a farewell from Laura. Please be seated while they sing. It may be these are the last songs we will hear from them for years."

I proudly led Laura to the steps and helped her up. Then I stepped to one side to drink in her beauty. I felt as if I should pinch myself to see if I were dreaming.

Harry beamed and bowed at Leah as he helped her up the steps.

The sisters started to sing. They sounded like nightingales as the thought began to sink deeper into my brain that I was a married man now and there was my beautiful bride singing and looking like an angel. Oh, how I loved her.

After several shouts for more and several encores from the sisters, the dance music finally started.

I didn't get to dance with Laura much as the evening continued. It seemed every man and boy in the building had to say farewell to her and enjoy her company for one last dance.

While Laura was dancing with her admirers I got to dance with Leah and received congratulations from many of the people there. Some of them I did not know by name but I had seen nearly all of them before either at the dances or in church. I was offered a drink by more than one of the revellers but I wasn't much for that anymore, and I knew Laura would not approve, so I politely declined. I'd never forgotten that experience in the saloon with Roy and some of the boys.

Chapter VIII

It was long past midnight when the dance let
out and much later before Laura and I could leave.
Finally our friends had gone home and the hall
was locked up. We left the presents there, having
decided to pick them up in our new wagon Sunday
afternoon. When we reached Laura's home we took
our shoes off and sneaked in quietly. Everyone else
was in bed. Mrs. Bybe had left a lamp on the
kitchen table close to some sandwiches and a
pitcher of cool milk. The food tasted good, especially
the milk. We silently slipped up the stairs to
Laura's room.

At church the next day Laura received more
good wishes and congratulations from those who
had not gone to the dance and wedding. Everyone
was very sincere in what they said to her. She had
been a part of their lives and they would miss her.
I'm sure they knew that she would miss them but
she was too excited to think much about that.

We straightened everything up at the dance hall
Sunday afternoon and packed most of our things in

preparation for our farewell the next morning. Roy helped me all he could, but when I suggested he come with me to get my new saddle horse he said he had an errand to run and would meet me at our bunkhouse later. I had a few things there to pick up.

I took enough money with me to finish paying for my horse and walked to the livery stable. Dan, the livery man, was waiting for me. I held out the $65.00 due him but he only shook his head. Instead he handed me the reins.

"The horse is all paid for," he said. "Roy paid off the balance. Said it was a wedding present."

I was speechless for a minute. I knew Roy was a generous guy, but I didn't expect him to give me a horse and saddle for a wedding present.

When I rode Blackie up to the boarding house to get my things and to thank Roy, he was not there. The only other place I could imagine he would be, at the time, was in the saloon, so I went down there. Sure enough, he was talking with some other men at the bar. When I stepped inside he spotted me.

"Wil," he yelled and motioned for me to come over. "Have one last drink with me. Don't know when I'll see you again."

"Nah, not this time," I said, remembering the last time Roy bought me a drink. I didn't say anything about the horse. When we finished I asked him to come with me to get the rest of my clothes. He followed me outside to where Blackie was tied.

"Roy, I want to pay you for the horse," I insisted. "You can't give me a horse and saddle. That's too much."

"Now look, Wil," he said, looking me straight in the eye. "It's my money, and to buy a horse for a good friend is what I wanted to do. Besides, if I hadn't spent it on your horse, I'd probably have lost it playing poker."

"Thanks," I said, finally deciding to accept the horse and saddle. "We hope you will come see us when you're down our way."

"I'll do it. You can bet on that."

He asked me to stop and see his family when we passed through Circle Valley. I promised him we would. We shook hands, I mounted Blackie and rode up the street. Roy had been the best friend I had ever had and I knew I'd miss him.

The next morning when we finished loading the wagon I went to the barn to get the horses. Mr. Bybe came to help. I led the team out to the wagon and tied Blackie to the tail gate, then hitched up the team. As I walked around the team I saw Mr. Bybe tying his bay mare to the back of the wagon near Blackie. He looked at me and smiled.

"Laura always liked Babe so you take her along," he said. "This saddle is the one I bought for Laura on her sixteenth birthday."

Laura was both surprised and pleased when she saw the bay mare tied to our wagon.

"Oh, Daddy," she said, as she hugged him. "Thanks so much. I'll take good care of her." By this time everyone was gathered around the wagon to say good-bye.

I climbed up on the wagon seat and reached down to help Laura up.

"We'll send you word when we get located," I said. "Hope you can visit us soon. Thanks for everything." I picked up the lines and clucked at the horses.

When we drove up the dugway that led from the little valley to the sagebrush flats above, Laura stood up and waved to her family. They were standing by the back porch, watching until we were out of sight.

The tears were streaming down Laura's face. I guessed she was homesick already. I stopped the team so she could get a good look at the home where she had grown up. I wasn't sure when we would return and I knew she would miss it. While the team waited, I turned and looked back too. I could understand Laura's feelings for I could still remember some of my loneliness when we left our old home in the midwest.

Finally I stood up by her and put my arm around her. We stood there looking back at the town that had been her home since she was born. When gold was discovered, miners came from all directions, some hoping to strike it rich, others only looking for a place to work and play. A few farmers came but they were in the minority.

All of the tents that had lined the little stream were now gone but I could envision them lined up on both sides of the creek, from the Sevier River on the east to the foothills in the west. I was sure some of them had been pitched up close to the higher mines. They were all gone now and homes dotted the little town in a planned, symmetrical way with streets running north and south, east and west. Because the little valley was narrow, the streets running north and south were very short.

Only the lucrative mines were still in operation. Many of the early claims failed but the big veins were still producing valuable ore.

One thing that worried me was the realization that I really didn't know where we were going and where we would live. I did know that our new home would be much different than the big white home that Laura was forsaking for me.

The more I thought about it, the more sorry I felt for Laura. I knew she loved her big home and I didn't blame her. It was the prettiest home I had ever been in. It was one of those large two-story buildings with lots of windows and two big porches running the full width of the house on both ends. The inside was furnished with beautiful, thick rugs partly covering the shiny hardwood floors. Pictures hung in appropriate places. Curtains hung at all the windows. Mrs. Bybe had the newest kitchen devices available in the west.

I wondered how Laura could leave all that to go wandering through half-settled wasteland inhabited mostly by Indians. I knew I loved her more than anything in the world but it was hard for me to understand that she could love me that much. I decided she probably did, or she wouldn't be in my wagon heading south that day. Well, it was too late for either one of us to change our minds. Besides, I had no intention of changing mine. I loved her and I was going to hang on to her as long as I could.

"Are you sorry?" I teased.

"Of course not, silly. I've just never moved away from home before and I know I'll miss my family. As soon as they are out of sight, I'll be all right."

When we reached the top of the dugway and started across the flats, Laura sat down. She was still crying. I put my arm around her and told her I loved her, and hoped I would be able to show her just how much I really cared.

She sat in the seat leaning against me. She looked so sweet in her new gingham dress and new sun bonnet. I hugged her tight and tried to console her. I felt sorry for taking her away from the friends and places she loved so much but I knew I would never be content to stay in the mines.

As I looked across that rolling sagebrush bench in front of us, I wondered what we were getting into. The sagebrush extended from the foothills on the right, to the river and then across to the hills on the left. The land looked empty and lonely and yet the sun was shining brightly and the air was clear and fresh. I breathed deeply and clucked at the team to hurry along for I knew there was a new life, and my family, waiting for us somewhere up ahead.

We followed the dirt road over one little flat after another. I kept watching for the small stream that they said was flowing from the west. It was almost noon when we reached it. We stopped for lunch where we could water the horses and let them rest while they ate some hay.

Laura took care of the riding horses while I tended to the team, then she fixed a bite of lunch and we talked about our future.

As we sat there in the shade of the wagon listening to the stillness of the midday, broken only by the gurgling of the little stream and the horses munching on their feed, I thought I was the happiest man on earth.

Late that afternoon after we had traveled through Circle Valley we rounded a little hill that jutted out from the western foothills. Looking ahead we could see a few farm houses. The one nearest to us was on our right. Part of it was dug into the hill. Further on we saw one in the middle of the narrowing valley, and on the right, close to the foothills was a log cabin with young poplar trees around it.

"That must be Roy's house," I said.

We drove up the little lane to the yard gate. I handed Laura the lines and jumped to the ground. Walking to the cabin door, I knocked.

"Come in," said a woman's voice from inside. As I opened the door I could see a woman fixing the night's meal.

"Are you Mrs. Parker?" I asked.

"Yes, I am," she said. "Won't you come in?"

I told her I had been working in the mines in Marysvale with her son.

"You mean Bob?" she asked as her eyes lit up.

"I knew him as Roy. I hope we are talking about the same person."

"Yes, we are," she replied. "Sometimes he likes to be called Roy. How is he? We haven't heard from him for so long."

I handed her the fifty dollars Roy had sent with me. A little boy and girl came running across the room and hid behind their mother.

"I wish he would stay closer to home and help his father, but he's so restless. I guess farming is not for him. Did he say anything about coming home?"

"Not exactly. He did say he thought he would leave the mines before long."

"I sure wish he would come home and help us around the farm. Are you alone?"

"No, my bride is in the wagon."

She followed me out the door toward the gate and the wagon.

We met Mr. Parker coming in from the corral. Mrs. Parker introduced us and told him that we had driven up from Marysvale that day. She also told him that I had been rooming and working with Bob.

He invited us to spend the night and I accepted.

We walked through the gate and I introduced them to Laura. I helped Laura down from the wagon.

"Mr. Halladay, drive your wagon in the yard," Mr. Parker said. "You can park it next to the house. That will keep it out of the wind later in the night. This canyon acts like a funnel some mornings."

I parked the wagon as he directed and he helped me unhitch my team. We put the horses in his barn, after removing the harnesses from the team and hanging them on the wagon.

By this time the older boys and girls started arriving home to help with the evening chores. We could easily tell where Roy got his nice personality. Everyone was friendly and pleasant.

While we ate the evening meal with the family they wanted to know all about Roy, the mines and our wedding. We had a good visit and found out to our satisfaction why Roy was such a generous person. They were thrilled to hear all the news about him. I had the feeling Roy would be better off at home with his family but he seemed to be such a free spirit that he just had to go his own way.

They said my family had gone up the canyon about a month earlier. I guessed Dad would be anxious to be on his way without us.

That night we slept in our covered wagon as we had our bed all fixed on the hay. Besides, the Parkers were crowded in their little cabin.

Chapter IX

Early the next morning, after eating breakfast with the Parkers, we headed up the rocky canyon road which was much rougher and slower than the one we had traveled the day before.

It was late in the afternoon when we drove out of the top end of the canyon into the meadows. We found my family camped on the south side of a ledge close to the meadows. They were anxiously awaiting my arrival. They were, of course, surprised to see me driving a wagon, but they were more surprised to see Laura sitting beside me.

Upon reaching the camp I jumped down from the wagon. Everyone rushed forward to greet me but their eyes were on Laura. It was really good to see them again. Ned and my two sisters had grown so much. They spoke to me but I could see their attention was still on Laura.

"I want you all to meet the most special girl in the world," I said, as I lifted Laura down from the wagon. "Mother, Dad, and the rest of you, I want you to meet my wife, Laura."

They all gasped.

"You certainly know how to pick a pretty one. Welcome, Laura," Dad said as he grabbed her and gave her a big hug. "I hope you will be very happy with Wil. He's a good boy."

"It really will be good to have you with us," Mother said as she put her arm around Laura and led her toward the tent. "You come with me. Supper will be ready soon and I know you're tired. That's a long way to travel in a bumpy wagon."

After my horses were unhitched and hobbled in the meadows we sat down to talk and plan. Father told me about the place he had found. He was anxious to get there before others did.

"Let's start in the morning then," I suggested. I thought if Nancy would help Laura drive the team, Ned and I could drive the cattle. We could put the wagon in the lead and if the cattle followed, Ned could handle them alone part of the time while I helped Laura. That would give Dad, Mother and Ellen time to pack things and catch up with us later in the day.

"Sounds great," Dad said. "We'll start in the morning then. I think the cattle are ready. If the calves get tired, we can put them in the wagons." With that settled the rest of the evening was spent catching up on all that had happened while we had been apart. But mainly everyone wanted to get to know Laura better, and to learn something about her family.

Early the next morning, we went to get our horses. We led them back to the wagons to harness and saddle them. When we were ready Laura and Nancy crawled up on the wagon seat ready to go. I tied Babe to the back of the wagon, picked up Blackie's reins and patted his neck. I put my left foot in the stirrup, reached up and grabbed the saddle horn and prepared to mount.

Blackie never even flicked an ear as I swung my right foot over his back and settled in the saddle. Ned was waiting for me. I leaned forward in the saddle and touched Blackie with my heels. "Let's go," I said.

Blackie's head went down and with one violent lunge he started for the clouds. I went up with him and kept right on going. By the time I lit, Blackie was halfway to the river with his hooves flying in all directions at once. I hit the ground with a thud, rolling over and over.

My hat came down close by, after sailing like a kite through the sky. I sat up and watched Blackie turn in the air and land on all four feet, suddenly stopping and looking straight back at me. He tossed his head up and down and whinnied.

Laura came running, asking if I was hurt, throwing her arms around me.

"Only my pride," I assured her, a little embarrassed.

"What happened?" she asked.

"I just touched him with my heels and he threw me farther than I have ever been thrown," I answered.

"But I thought he was broke to ride."

"That's what they said when I bought him," I sat there looking at Blackie.

Father had been watching. He started to laugh when he figured I was not hurt.

"Look at that beast," he said, pointing at the horse. "I think he's just saying hello."

"I wonder if he's the kind that has to get his exercise every morning before he can go to work," I said as I stood up, brushing myself off. I walked over to where Blackie stood, still tossing his head up and down.

"Well, old boy, let's see if you can do that again when I'm ready," I said to him.

"Be careful," Laura pleaded.

I took hold of the reins, tied them in a knot, threw them over his neck and prepared to mount again.

"Now that I know how you greet people, I'll be ready," I told him as I mounted. As before, Blackie stood still. I leaned forward as I had done the first time and said, "Let's go."

Blackie started out in a swinging lope as if nothing had ever happened. The rest of the family stood there gazing after us in amazement.

"Well, how about that?" Father laughed. "That horse has a personality all his own."

I waved for Ned to catch up as I continued riding towards the cattle.

"What do you think of him?" I asked as Ned reined Pete close to me.

"He looks great, but he sure surprised me," he answered.

"Me too. Now I don't know what's next. I suppose I'll have to watch him every morning. Some horses just have to get the kinks out before they get down to business."

We rode around the cattle, starting them towards camp. The calves were still too young to brand. I asked Ned if he knew where we were going.

"Southeast of here someplace," he said. "I haven't been there yet. We can ask Dad when we get back to camp."

I could see that we would have to drive the cattle slowly or put some of the younger calves in the wagons. We drove the stock to the road and stopped to see if everyone was ready.

"Where do we go from here?" I asked as Dad came towards us. Dad pointed up the valley to show me the direction we would go.

"When we get past Panguitch we can turn straight east or go on a little farther to a red canyon, then continue east to the east fork of the Sevier River," he explained. "Up along that stream the grass will make great summer range. Farther to the east are the breaks where the terrain drops down hundreds of feet. During the winter it will be mild down there, a good place for the stock during the cold months."

"Let's be on our way," I said as I clucked at Blackie and waved for Laura to lead out. She waved back at me, threw me a kiss and flipped the lines on the horses' backs. We were on our way.

Up the valley we plodded, moving the cattle as fast as we dared. The cows bawled and the calves answered. Our dreams were in front of us and we were confident about our future. I was sure Father had chosen the right place. The meadows we were leaving provided lots of green grass and I was sure the stock would do very well if they were left there for the summer.

Laura and Nancy continued in front with the wagon. Ned and I followed, driving the small herd of cattle. It was tedious and poky but I was enjoying every minute of it. It felt wonderful to be out in the open again, on a good horse.

After a couple of hours I asked Nancy to trade places with me. I didn't dare let her ride Blackie so I put her on Babe. We wrestled a couple of the smallest calves in the back of the wagon. The mother cows bawled and followed faster to keep up. That helped the whole herd move faster.

Before we stopped for noon, Dad and Mother caught us. They went on ahead to find a good spot to rest and to eat lunch. In the afternoon Laura rode

Babe and helped me while Ned and Nancy drove the wagon.

By the end of the second day we were almost to the entrance of the red canyon. A small clear stream flowed out of it. Father said we would not have any trouble going up through the canyon. Laura continued to ride Babe so she could enjoy the scenery better. She thought it was such a beautiful canyon.

I felt badly that I couldn't provide a better honeymoon for her but I knew she loved to ride horses and we were seeing new country every day. She loved that, and so did I.

Late the next day we left the canyon behind, moving across a wide, flat, sagebrush valley. It was bordered by trees to the south, but extended to the north as far as I could see. Northeast there was a tall pink mountain that ended sharply where the breaks started. The flat, sagebrush plateau looked like good cattle country.

The next day we reached the main stream of the East Fork of the Sevier River. The grass was plentiful and the water was clear and cool. There were tall trees on the nearby hills. The cattle would have plenty of shade during the hot days. We saw other cattle scattered up and down the valley. Other people had already settled in the area. We liked what we saw and decided to leave the cattle in this high country where they would get fat for fall.

Leaving the herd we moved on to the breaks. What we saw was breathtaking. To our left and right we saw colorful rocks, ravines and ledges of all shapes, sizes and colors. Laura seemed overwhelmed by the sheer beauty of it all. She dismounted and walked along the rim, soaking it in. The lowlands went on as far as the eye could see.

Dad jumped down from his wagon and checked his brakes. He suggested I do the same. I could tell from the looks of the narrow, winding dugway—it was more like a trail—that we would need good brakes. I wondered about a log drag but Dad doubted we would need them.

Dad said he would go first. Laura decided she would ride Babe, and Nancy wanted to ride Pete, so Ned got on Blackie and said he would follow me. I was glad the weather was good. I would hesitate to tackle that steep grade in a rainstorm.

It was not as bad going down as I thought it would be. Soon we were at the bottom of the dugway and from there on we followed the small stream and a few other wagon tracks down the canyon.

When we reached the little valley we could see that a few other settlers had already started building cabins. We proceeded to a spot on the upper edge of what we figured would someday be a town and decided to camp there by the stream that came down the west canyon. It was already sundown so we prepared for the night.

The next morning we visited some of the other settlers to find out where we could choose a farm and a place for our homes. We were told that where we were camped was unclaimed and all the land above us was open for settlement.

After riding up the canyon and looking around we decided to stake a claim for a farm at the upper end of the valley close to the beautiful, pink ledges and stake claims to two small pieces of land where the wagons were parked for our homes. We figured with the water from the canyon we could grow all kinds of crops including garden produce.

"Laura, what do you think of this place?" I asked her that night.

"It's warm down here now. I imagine it will be very pleasant in the winters," she responded. "When I look up at those colorful cliffs, I'm amazed at the natural beauty.

"But we're so far away from everybody," she continued, her countenance growing sad. "I guess I'll get used to that."

"It looks good to me," Ned volunteered.

"And what about you, Nancy?" I asked.

"We've been moving so much the last few years that any place where we can settle down looks all right to me. I'll bet Mother will be happy to light and stay put."

The next morning, Dad, Ned and I staked what we wanted for our town lots. Then we rode up the canyon and cut some posts for staking out the farm.

When we finally decided what we wanted, we put the posts into the ground for the corner boundaries of our property.

We figured we could plant a few crops as soon as we could plow the land. We could start on our houses and gardens while the crops were growing.

We worked from daylight till dark on the farm and soon had some wheat planted. Next we started on our homes. Logs were cut and trimmed and each day the walls grew higher and higher. We hoped that by the time the cold weather set in, the cabins would be comfortable and warm.

While we worked, the women tried to make life bearable in tents. I knew Mother was used to living in one but I wasn't sure Laura had ever been *in* one. She never complained, but I knew she was having a struggle trying to keep as clean as she was used to.

Laura and the girls carried rocks to dam the stream enough to form a pool where they could bathe. It wasn't like a tub full of hot water, but it was better than nothing.

Chapter X

During the summer, one of the men would ride up on the mountain to check the cattle every week. That responsibility usually fell to Ned. One morning as he was preparing to leave, he looked up at the mountain and wondered if there wasn't a shorter route than following the road. The road led north a few miles before it started up the canyon.

"If I could go straight up here, I ought to be able to save a lot of time," he said to himself. "The cattle should be almost directly west of here."

He wrapped a small lunch in his jacket and tied it to the back of his saddle. He climbed on Pete and started riding straight west up past our farm toward the rugged breaks that were so visible from our home.

We had built a road from our new cabins to the farm and there it stopped. Beyond the farm only a small trail was visible. It followed close to the stream. The oak brush was plentiful and pines dotted the rolling hills in all directions.

The dark green of the trees was a beautiful contrast to the colorful ledges. From some places the view was breathtaking, especially where the tall pines formed borders to the view beyond. When riding below the breaks I often stopped my horse to take in the sights, and Laura never seemed to satisfy her delight in looking at them. Often, she said she wished she were an artist and could capture what God had placed in front of us.

Up the stream Ned went, all the time trying to pick out the canyon that would lead to the top. By the time he reached the breaks, the little ravines ran in all directions, most ending at the base of steep ledges. He went from one to another with the same dead-end results.

Finally he followed the canyon running south parallel to the ledges. It had some water in it which Ned guessed started somewhere near the top where he wanted to go. He started up the canyon, realizing that if it didn't lead him all the way to the top, it would be too late to try something else until the following day.

After an hour, he stopped for a drink and to eat a sandwich. He sat at the edge of the stream looking at the ledges while Pete munched on green grass.

"What a horrible place to lose a cow," he thought. A cow could go from one ravine to another and never be found.

As he sat there, he noticed the majestic rock spires standing like people and buildings. He could pick out castles and churches. Some ledges looked like kings and queens. The colors were red, orange, pink, white, yellow and even some blue and green hues.

"It may be beautiful to look at, but how do I get through it?" he asked his horse.

Getting back on Pete he continued on. He saw some cougar tracks along the stream bed. He wondered what the big cat was up to, probably stalking some kind of game. He hoped the cat wouldn't get a hunger for veal.

A little farther on he saw wolf tracks and then some coyote footprints. Just then he looked ahead and saw something move out of the stream bed. When he reached the spot where he had seen the movement he found the partially eaten body of a small deer. Pete snorted and pricked up his ears. When they reached the dead deer, Ned saw many tracks around it.

He guessed the cat had probably killed the deer, the wolves and coyotes coming later. He figured the movement he had seen had been one of the coyotes.

The shadows from the ledges began to grow long, and Ned was still looking for a place to reach the top. Finally he stopped.

"I think we're on a wild goose chase, Pete," he said as he patted the sweating horse. "Not much sense starting back this late, or going any farther tonight. Let's find a high bank or rock where we can build a fire near some good grass and camp for the night."

They found a good spot and Ned unsaddled Pete and hobbled him in the nearby grass. He built a fire close to an overhanging rock and settled down for the night. He placed the saddle near the rock where he could use it as a pillow and near enough to the fire so his feet would keep warm. He untied his coat and pulled it over him. The saddle blanket was under him. He figured he wouldn't sleep much, but at least he would be comfortable.

As he lay there he looked up at the stars and listened to the stillness of the night being broken only by the yelping of the coyotes. He was glad he had Pete close by. If anything came around, Pete would snort and wake him up. He pulled his rifle out of its scabbard and laid it by his side, his hand on it.

When he thought about it, he was surprised that he had not seen any signs of Indians that day. He guessed they had better sense than to ride up in this forsaken country.

When my father came in for supper with the milk, it was getting dark. He asked Mother and the girls if they had seen Ned. They hadn't.

"He should be back," Dad continued. "I hope nothing has happened. Maybe he had to look for some of the strays. Cattle don't always stay together. Maybe he had to round some of them up. He should be here before too long. I guess we shouldn't worry."

Dad and Mother fretted all night waiting for Ned to return. He had never stayed all night before.

"If he isn't here by daylight, I'm going after him," Dad decided.

By daylight Dad was at my house. He asked me to go with him, knowing I was a good tracker.

We were soon on our way up the road heading towards the mountain. I watched for Pete's tracks. As the morning light grew brighter, I watched more carefully. Finally I stopped and dismounted. Carefully, I inspected all tracks leading in both directions.

"Dad, Pete hasn't been up this road lately," I concluded. "I don't think there were any horses on it yesterday at all."

"Are you sure?" he asked.

"I put shoes on him the other day and I know he hasn't been along here lately," I answered.

"Then where did he go?"

"The other day we were talking about a shorter route to the mountain top. We wondered if it were possible to ride up the canyon past our farm and find a way through those breaks. They seemed so rough and steep no one had ever attempted it. I have a feeling Ned might have tried to go that way. We'd better check to be sure," I suggested.

"If you think he might have gone that way," Dad said. "You go ahead and double check. I'll continue up the road and maybe we will meet on top. I could even meet him coming down the canyon. If you don't find his tracks, come on back home and I'll see you tonight." He kicked his horse in the ribs.

I turned Blackie down the road. I thought I had a better chance of finding Ned than Dad did.

Chapter XI

I rode back past town and started up the lane that led to our farm. Sure enough, Pete's tracks were in the dusty road. Now I was sure what Ned had done.

I followed Pete's tracks into the deep gullies and cliffs. In some places the walls were so close together that one could hardly ride between them. I decided it would take too long to trace every step, so I rode out away from the ledges, going farther upstream before I circled back towards them.

When I reached the little stream that led south, parallel to the ledges, I ran on to Ned's tracks again. I let Blackie drink and quenched my own thirst. The water was refreshing and looked as clear as a piece of glass. Although the stream was small, the wash was wide, indicating there had been huge spring runoffs, or flash floods following summer thunder showers. It was hard to believe that a little stream like that could turn into a raging torrent.

The sun was up and the day was warm and still. I noticed the beautiful colors of the ledges and thought what a good place this would be for cattle thieves to hide, especially if there was a trail leading to the top.

All of a sudden dark clouds appeared over the cliffs. I knew this was no place to be in a cloudburst. I hoped the clouds would just pass over.

I urged my horse into a trot, trying to gain as much distance as I could in the event it started to rain. All at once I saw a sheet of water spilling over the cliffs. Though I was still dry, I knew it was raining in the high country at the head of the canyon. I knew I had to find a place to climb out of the gully before the flood came.

I could see Ned's tracks leading up the stream, but when the rain started to come down in torrents, I knew I had to get out of there in a hurry. Just ahead I saw a small ravine leading to the left away from the cliffs and main gully. I urged Blackie towards it.

As the horse churned through the wet sand towards the side exit, I thought I caught a glimpse of something dark coming down the main gully in a hurry. I stopped.

It was Pete and Ned. Right behind them I could see a wall of water bearing down on them.

"Ned," I yelled as loud as I could. I waved for him to hurry.

Ned looked up and saw me. He had been riding with his head down trying to protect his face from the rain. He waved at me and kicked Pete in the sides to hurry faster.

"Hurry!" I yelled, waving frantically. I wasn't sure he knew how close the flood was behind him. I knew we had only seconds to reach the high ground in the side canyon. I started up the bank. Blackie stumbled and slid as he struggled to keep his balance. Pete was having the same trouble, his feet sliding in all directions at once.

Ned glanced over his shoulder as Pete was battling to gain higher ground while maintaining his footing. By now the water was tearing at Pete's back legs trying to pull him downward into the thick, muddy, relentless current.

Ned had been so lulled by the roar of the storm that he never knew the flood was behind him.

"Go! Pete, go!" Ned screamed as he leaned forward and kicked the little horse in the sides again and again.

Pete floundered and fell. Ned scrambled to the ground holding onto the reins with one hand and grabbing the nearest juniper with the other.

"Wil!" he yelled as loud as he could.

I unbuckled the strap that held my lariat, and in a flash threw the loop over Pete's head and wrapped the rope around my saddle horn.

"Back," I yelled at Blackie and pulled on the reins. Blackie leaned into the rope, frantically trying to maintain his footing in the slippery mud. In a quick move, Ned slipped the reins out of the loop so the lariat could tighten on Pete's neck. After getting the reins free, Ned started pulling again as hard as he could. Between his pulling and Blackie's help we gradually pulled the floundering little horse up over the slick bank onto better footing. Pete struggled to his feet much to the relief of Ned and me.

Ned slipped the rope off Pete's neck and we scrambled up the side of the little ravine to the top of a small ridge where we would be safe from the floods.

I dismounted and we crawled under a small tree. The rain continued to pour down in torrents, and soon most of the gooey mud washed off Pete's heaving sides.

"Whew-w-w, that was close," I said, breathing easier.

"Thanks, Wil," Ned said. "I didn't know the flood was so close. The lightening and thunder were so loud I couldn't hear anything else. If you hadn't been in the right place at the right time, we would have been goners. Remind me never to come up here in a rainstorm again."

The horses turned their backs toward the storm and held their heads near the ground close to our little tree. Every time the lightening flashed or the thunder roared, the sounds bounced back and forth through the canyons and steep cliffs, magnifying the noise to a deafening roar. The horses would flinch and stomp.

"Hang on to your bridle reins," I cautioned. "We don't want the horses to get spooked and break away. If they get under a big tree they could be struck by lightening."

"I'd surely hate to lose Pete after what we've been through the last two days," he said.

I asked him if he had found a shorter route to the top.

"No," he said. "I've ridden for miles up this stream bed and it all looks the same—just tall, sturdy ledges. If there's a trail to the top, I couldn't find it."

I told him how Dad and I had set out to find him when he hadn't come home. I told him how worried Dad had been.

"I'm powerful hungry," Ned said. "I've had only one sandwich since breakfast yesterday and I'm starved. I wish I had part of that venison I saw yesterday,"

We talked about the cougars, wolves and coyotes and the colorful ledges all around us.

The hours passed and finally the rain stopped. Late in the afternoon the streambeds had drained to the point where we figured we could start back.

It was after dark when we reached town. We were relieved to find Dad had arrived ahead of us.

Chapter XII

One sunny Sunday afternoon shortly following the flash flood, I saddled both of our horses and led them to our back door.

"Come on, Laura," I called through the door. "I have a surprise for you."

She stepped outside and looked at me standing there holding the bridle reins.

"I want you to see some of the most beautiful country in the world," I explained.

"Will we be gone long?"

"Probably," I said, smiling. "Maybe we'll be home by dark."

Laura loved to ride horses and I knew she would take me up on my offer. Quickly she disappeared into the house to change out of her dress. When she walked out she was wearing high-topped shoes, a white blouse and her flared-hipped riding pants. She never rode side saddle and I didn't blame her. Her pink cheeks accentuated her bright eyes as she quickly mounted her little mare.

"Lead the way, General," she said, excitement in her voice.

We rode up the little valley past our new farm where some of the young wheat was showing promise of developing into a good harvest. As we neared the colored cliffs Laura stared from one to another.

"Aren't they just beautiful, Wil," she exclaimed, never taking her eyes off them. I led her from one box canyon to another while she just sat in her saddle and gazed in awe as her horse followed mine.

After about an hour, I stopped in a shady spot near a clear little spring. We dismounted. I reached up to help her down.

"How do you like this country?" I asked.

"It's fantastic," she exclaimed, without even looking at me. "I can see so many forms and shapes. It's almost as if some master sculpture had spent his life carving them. I hope we can come here often." She finally looked at me and smiled. "Can we come here every Sunday for a picnic?"

"Anytime you want," I assured her.

It was almost sundown before I could get her to head for home and the chores. It made me happy that she loved the area so much. I also had marveled at the variety of beauty and shapes and I knew we would return often.

That summer, for six days every week, we chopped logs, then dragged them to our lots or to the saw mill to trade for boards. We took care of our farms and gardens and built cabins by the side of the stream.

As the weeks went by we finally completed the log walls of our future homes and started on the roofs. It took all three of us to brace and nail the rafters. After that we could handle many of the jobs alone.

In time the roofs were completed and the women helped us chink between the logs. We left the floors till last, knowing we could work on them during bad weather. By early fall we had to stop building and harvest our first crop of grain while the women bottled and preserved food for winter.

The women worked well together. Mother taught Laura and my two sisters the fine art of storing foods.

One evening I rode down from the farm, unsaddled and put my horse in the corral. I knew I must build a shed, at least for our milk cow and horses, to protect them from the winter storms.

I had in mind how to build it, but I also knew that I must continue to make our home more comfortable. I knew it wasn't much of a home, only a log cabin divided into two rooms. Someday I would build some adjoining rooms, but right now I wanted to improve what we had. Laura had been used to a much bigger and better place.

We set up our cook stove in the south room along with a table and chairs. I built some shelves in one corner where Laura could keep her dishes and food. The other room was used as our bedroom. Near the bed I drove some wooden pegs in a log to hang our clothes on. Laura owned more clothes than I did, so I helped her put some long pegs in one of the logs so she could hang a piece of cloth on it to cover her dresses and protect them from most of the dust. It wasn't much of a clothes closet but it helped.

The two windows, one on each side of the door, had no glass in them, yet. When cool weather set in we would have to cover them with cloth until I could get some window glass. As long as it was warm the window openings allowed light and fresh air into the small cabin.

At the first sign of snow on the mountain all of the ranchers went after their cattle. We drove them down and herded them into the lower valleys and canyons where there was water and good winter feed. They weren't far below our new community and we would be able to check on them often during the winter months.

Our lives were happy and we kept building fences, corrals and sheds. Whenever anyone from our area traveled anywhere, they always brought back fruit trees, shrubs and berry bushes to enrich our lives. All the settlers wanted to make our community a good place to live. We built a town hall where we could hold church and dances. As new settlers moved in, we helped them build their homes.

The next spring we all went together to bring our cattle in for branding and to move them up to the summer range. The stock had weathered the winter in good condition, proving that Dad had been right about the quality of the winter range in the lower canyons. The little snow that reached the lower elevations never lasted long. We all enjoyed the mildness of the winter. We felt like we had settled in the right place.

I knew, however, that the pioneering was hard on Laura, but Mother and my two sisters always seemed to be around when I was gone, for which I was very grateful.

One day the next summer, Ned came back from checking on the cattle with the news many of us in the valley had feared. Cattle rustlers had driven some of our stock away. He guessed they had taken about twenty head. He didn't know whose cattle were gone—all the herds mixed together when loose on the range.

We notified other ranchers and early the next morning we headed up the road. Ned led us to the tracks where the cattle had been driven north and on to where the tracks mixed in with a bigger herd.

Cattle rustling was something we all worried about but hoped would never happen. Rustling could take all our gain and profit for the year. The rustlers never seemed to take everything. They always left enough so there would be more animals to steal the next year. None of us would be able to build a herd if the rustling continued, and there was always the possibility that the rustling could break us. Something had to be done.

Claud Packard said he bet it was Jesse Challis and his gang. I had heard of Challis but I had never met him.

As we studied the signs on the ground we could see where little groups of cattle had been brought into this meadow from all directions. I guess the rustlers figured that if they took a small number from each area, the rustling would not be discovered until fall, or maybe not at all.

Some of the men wanted to go after the rustlers, but cooler heads knew it would be better to bring in the law. Otherwise someone might get hurt.

That night I sat down and wrote a letter to the Utah Territorial Governor telling him what had happened and asking for help. I knew it would be weeks before we received any answer.

One day about two weeks later a tall rawboned man came riding into town. He rode a lanky, sorrel, stocking-legged horse, and was leading a pack mule. He had my letter with him, so he was directed to my place.

It was almost sundown when he reached my home. I had been up to the farm watering a new crop of oats and was returning to do the evening chores. I saw him dismount at my front gate so I rode over to him.

"Can I help you?" I asked. "My name is Wil Halladay."

"My name is John Holden," he said, reaching out to shake my hand. "Is this your letter?" He handed me the letter.

"Yes, it's mine," I answered.

"The Governor sent me down to see if something can be done. I'd like to meet with all of the ranchers right away."

"We can meet at the town hall tonight," I responded. "My brother will help get the word out."

"Fine," he answered. "I'll pitch camp up along the creek."

"No, you stay with us," I insisted. "Bring the horses in here and put them in the stalls. We'll eat supper together and then go to the meeting."

John offered no further objection, but followed me through the gate. I helped him put his horses away for the night then hurried in the house to tell Laura that we would have company that night. Laura was glad because we didn't get many visitors. Now she could hear what was happening in the world around us.

That evening John and I walked to the hall together. When all the ranchers arrived, I stood and introduced John. He stepped up to the front of the room and told the men that he had been sent

100

here by the territorial governor in answer to my letter. He told us the Governor was aware that more people were moving into the southern part of the territory, and more state officers were needed to combat the cattle rustling and Indian problems.

"I have been authorized to appoint someone if we can find the right man," he said.

"Who is the right man?" Father asked.

"I heard there's a man down here who's been a lawman before," he said. "If I can find him, he can start immediately. His name is Claud Packard."

"He's sitting right over there," Dad said as he pointed at Claud. "But we didn't know he was a lawman."

"What about it, Claud? Will you do it?" John asked.

Claud stood up, slowly.

"Yes, I've been a lawman, but I am too old for that now," he said. "I know what's expected and it should be a younger man. I've got a recommendation, if you want to hear it."

"Go ahead," John urged.

"How about Wil Halladay? He's energetic, levelheaded and he can track like an Indian. I'll be glad to help him all I can."

All eyes turned toward me. I was dumbfounded. I didn't know what to say. John turned to look at me too.

"Well, Mr. Halladay, what do you say? If you're as good as Mr. Packard says, I can swear you in right here and we can start investigating these cattle raids immediately."

"I don't know," I said. "I wasn't expecting this at all." I looked at Dad. He seemed almost as surprised as I was. The men started encouraging me to take it. They said they would back me up. Finally I said yes, so John administered the oath to me in front of them all. Then he pinned a badge on me. When we started for home I was still trying to think things through.

I worried about how Laura would handle this new assignment. She was expecting our first baby later in the summer and I didn't want to leave her alone. But we could sure use the money. I knew Mother and the girls would help all they could. If it hadn't been for my family being near, I probably wouldn't have consented to take the job.

As John, Dad, Ned and I walked toward home I was worried that maybe I had made the wrong decision. When we reached home, Laura was asleep so I didn't wake her. I figured I'd tell her in the morning.

There wasn't much sleep for me that night. I worried about the responsibility I had accepted. I wanted to do what I could to stop the rustling. The other ranchers were struggling like we were. The continued theft of our cattle could mean failure for us all.

During breakfast the next morning I told Laura about the meeting.

"Someone has to do it," I explained. "And it will bring us some needed cash."

John saddled his horse early and headed out, telling me that if I needed any help to be sure and let him know. He reminded me that I could get help from Claud and the other cattlemen. He wished me good luck.

I felt more than a little lonely when he left. I knew I had assumed a great responsibility. I was glad our town marshal would be around.

The year moved along rather smoothly. No more rustling took place that summer, but we still knew we had to be more alert, especially me. We had to check the cattle more often.

Chapter XIII

One evening, early in September, after Ned and I had been working on a shed and corral near the bottom corner of the farm, we started for home to do chores. As we rounded a short turn in the lane we came face to face with a stranger sitting on his horse. The oak brush was thick on both sides of the road, and as Ned and I had been talking, neither one of us had heard the other rider.

I stopped Blackie, wondering who the man was and what he wanted. Few riders ever rode up that way. He sat there looking at us. He was tanned from many days in the sun and wind. His black hair hung down over his collar. He sat straight in his saddle while his hands relaxed on the saddle horn. I guess he had heard us talking and decided to wait in the middle of the road.

"Are you Wil Halladay?" he asked, after looking from Ned to me.

"Yes, I am," I answered. "Can I help you?"

"I think you can," he replied. "John Holden told me about you. My name is Jacob Hamblin." He threw his left leg over the front of his saddle around the horn. "John says you are a good tracker and have some know-how in conversing with our red brethren."

"I like to think I can track pretty well, but from what I've heard, no one understands the Indian languages better than Jacob Hamblin."

"What I need right now is some one to help me capture a troublemaker. He's been rustling horses and has set fire to a ranch shed. If they catch him, they might string him up and we don't want that. Will you help me?"

I liked his approach and had heard so many good comments about him and his work with the Indians that I felt I could not say no. I told him I would help him, then asked when we would leave.

He smiled at me. "In the morning will be fine," he replied.

I introduced him to Ned, then invited him to come home with us. I was sure Laura would like to meet him, and hear what news he had brought with him. Outside news was always scarce down our way.

As we started down the lane, I turned to him. "Where do you think this Indian is and how many men does he have with him?"

"From what I understand, he may be along the San Juan River and he only has one companion— his son. The other Indians don't like what he's doing and wish he would stop. He won't listen to them and wants to fight everybody. I'd like to catch him alive and maybe talk some sense into him."

He told me we would travel light and he expected we would be back in a week or so. At daylight we were ready to leave.

I didn't like to leave Laura for very long, but I knew my family would watch out for her. Still, I would miss her. I remembered when we were married thinking that a man could never love a woman more than I loved Laura, but as the months passed that love continued to deepen. It seemed nearly every day I enjoyed being with her more than the day before. I was sure her love was deepening too. It seemed there was nothing she wouldn't do for me. There was no doubt in my mind but what the love I shared with Laura was the single most important thing in my life.

After saying goodbye to Laura, Hamblin and I headed down the canyon. We were headed to Lee's Ferry to check for any sign of the Indian there. From there we intended to head east towards the San Juan River and Bluff, where the main trouble was taking place.

No one at Lee's Ferry had seen the Indians but they had heard of the raids. They had heard too that the Indian we were after, Josey, now called himself the Fire Warrior.

We continued to Bluff. There we contacted the town marshal, a Mr. Lyman. He told us he had been trying to catch Josey too, but had failed so far.

"Do they seem to follow a pattern?" I asked.

"I think they do," Mr. Lyman answered. "The first place they raided was up river, about five miles above town. Almost a week later they struck the next ranch further up. I am wondering if they are ready to hit the next ranch above that."

"Sounds reasonable," I agreed. "What do they do?"

"They just sneak in and steal all the horses they can get their hands on," he responded. "Before leaving the first place they set a shed on fire. I tracked them to a box canyon where I stopped. It was such a natural spot for an ambush that I came back. I would rather capture them before they reach their hideout." He drew a map, showing where the ranches were in relation to the suspected hideout.

"Do you know Josey?" the sheriff asked.

"Yes," Hamblin replied. "And I think I can persuade him to stop these raids if I can get hold of him. Do either of you have an idea how we can do it?"

"I think I might," I volunteered.

"Good. Let's hear it."

"I think Marshal Lyman is right," I began. "There seems to be a pattern developing and they may be ready to strike the next ranch. They know the marshal is after them, but they're not afraid of him because he won't go in the canyon after them.

They are probably thinking that if they can steal enough horses, the whites will give up and leave."

I paused and looked at the two older more experienced men, wondering if I was overstepping my bounds.

"Continue," Mr. Lyman said.

"Jacob and I will ride up the canyon for a few miles where we'll stop along the river in the tall willows and hide. At the same time the marshal could ride out to the last ranch that was attacked, then begin riding home. The Indians would see him returning and figure they were clear to raid the next ranch. The marshal would join us after dark, and together we would ride to the ranch that hadn't yet been raided, and be ready for them if and when they arrive." I paused, waiting for their reactions.

"Should they come to steal horses," Hamblin asked, "how do you propose we catch Josey and the boy?"

I told them we only needed to catch one of the Indians, not both. I thought that if we caught the boy, Josey would try to negotiate the boy's release. This would give Hamblin the opportunity he was looking for to talk to Josey. If Josey was the one we caught, the boy probably wouldn't continue the raiding without his father's leadership.

"Probably so," Mr. Lyman agreed.

"Then let's hope they're ready to strike again tonight," I said.

Mr. Hamblin looked at me. "Just how do you plan on capturing one of them, Mr. Halladay?"

"Seems to me," I began, "that if we could reach the ranch without being seen and hide our horses below the ranch in the river willows, we could sneak into the corrals and sheds where we could be hidden from sight, armed with our lariats. We could rope one of them when they slip in to open the gate."

"They might have guns," Mr. Hamblin warned.

"I don't think either one of them is carrying anything but a bow and arrow," the marshal said. "No one has reported any shooting. They seem to like the quiet approach. Just arrows."

"As soon as we rope one of them," I continued, "we must act quickly to prevent his escape. He will probably have a knife and attempt to cut the rope free. The two who didn't rope him will have to get the knife away."

"Let's try it," Hamblin said. "I'd like to settle this whole thing peacefully before someone gets hurt."

Marshal Lyman told us to meet him up the river in a thick willow patch about ten o'clock that night. The Marshal started up the road, hoping Josey would be watching.

We relaxed until about nine o'clock, then headed up the river, staying in or near the willows as much as possible.

Upon finding the marshal on his return journey, we hurried to the ranch arriving shortly after midnight. We were still in the thick willows and close to the river.

We climbed off our horses and tied them to the willows. We quickly untied our lariats and followed the marshal to the corral fence. Horses were inside. Some of them were milling around. I guessed they wanted to be out in the pastures. I crept along the fence to the right until I reached the gate the Indians would have to use to get the horses out. Hamblin and the marshal vanished in the darkness.

I wanted to stay close to the gate so I moved back along the fence. Just inside the corral, lay a large horse, resting. I spoke to him, softly. He didn't move. Hoping he wouldn't be afraid, I climbed through the fence just in front of him and stationed myself between the horse and a big post. It seemed like a good place to hide. If someone came to steal horses I would be in place to throw a loop as soon as the gate opened. From where I was I could easily reach any intruder with my rope. I did not know where the other two men were hidden but I knew they were close.

After standing beside the post for most of an hour, straining my sight and hearing, I gradually slid down to a sitting position. I figured no one would see me that close to the horse. Besides the moon was only a sliver of light in the west and the bright stars didn't give enough light to make any difference. I knew the dim shadows of the poles and fence posts would obscure my hiding place.

We waited for what seemed an eternity. I was sure we had picked the wrong night. I wondered when the next attack might be, if not tonight. I wondered if they might be attacking another ranch while we waited in hiding at this one.

The air was still, but not chilly. I began to relax. Then I heard a slight sound to my right. Slowly turning my head, I caught a glimpse of a figure opening the gate ever so carefully.

My hand tightened on my lariat and I began to wonder just how I was going to stand up without being discovered. The man opened the gate wide and carefully walked toward the shed that covered the west end of the corral. I guessed he wanted to get all the horses he could.

I sat rigid until a horse passed between me and him. Then I stood up, silently. With my rope ready, I waited until the horse passed. The man was less than twenty feet from me. I flipped my rope towards him. As I did so I saw a movement on top of the shed as a second loop shot forward from that direction. Both ropes landed at the same time on the surprised man. I jerked and the marshal on top of the shed jerked too. We had caught our horse thief by surprise and the Indian fell to the ground, groaning and swearing in his native tongue. We pulled our ropes tighter while Hamblin hustled in to help. He grabbed the partly bound Indian and held him down until we could get to him. The three of us tied our victim's hands behind his back and led him out of the corral.

By then most of the horses had scattered. We didn't worry, knowing we could round them up later. I was pleased my plan had worked.

With the Indian's hands tied behind his back and our lariat ropes around his body, we led him outside of the corral. He continued to struggled and grumble against us and the ropes.

Hamblin took hold of the Indian's shoulders and looked directly into his eyes.

"Josey," he said, "Why are you doing this? You know your people want peace. They don't want trouble anymore. You know that. Now why are you doing this?"

"This Indian land. White man must go," the Indian answered.

"Josey, you know there is plenty of land for all," Hamblin continued. "I have met with your chief. We have always tried to be your friends. Isn't that true?"

Josey ducked his head and would not answer. Hamblin took hold of his chin and turned his face so he could look into Josey's eyes.

"Answer me, Josey. Haven't we always tried to be your friends? Haven't we shared our food with your people? Haven't we tried to teach you better ways to raise and preserve food?"

"White man must go."

"No, we're not leaving. We're going to stay and be your friends whether you want us to or not." Hamblin let loose of Josey and turned to look out across the dark landscape.

"I'll tell you what," Hamblin said as he turned to Josey again. "If you will promise me that you will stop making trouble and go back to your tribe, I'll let you go. If you won't, then we are going to lock you up in jail. I know you don't want that. What do you say?"

"My son get me free," he bragged.

"No he won't," Hamblin said. "He is only following you. If you will go straight, he will too. How about it?"

"We burn white man lodges," Josey threatened.

"If that's your answer, then we'll lock you up until you can think straight. Where's your horse?" Hamblin asked as he started leading Josey up the lane.

Josey would not say any more, so Hamblin asked the marshal and me to bring our horses up from the river. He said he'd lead Josey up to the road. He was sure we would find the Indian's horse there.

"What about the boy? Do you think he'll cause any trouble?" I asked.

"No, I don't think so," Hamblin said. "He'll probably stay around but without his father leading him, I think he'll behave." I headed down to the river to get the horses.

The faint shadows were ghostly and I moved cautiously. I knew there was another Indian around, and I didn't want to be taken by surprise.

When I returned with our mounts, Josey was still refusing to cooperate. We got on the horses and continued up the lane toward the road. That's when we heard a horseman riding toward the hills. I was sure it was the boy heading for his hideout.

We couldn't find Josey's horse, finally deciding the boy took it with him. We caught one of the rancher's horses and tied Josey on it.

As we headed for the town jail to lock Josey up, I kept thinking how patient Hamblin had been. He kept talking to Josey as if this Indian was a close friend, or a son. I couldn't help but feel that Hamblin had a great love for these people.

With our prisoner locked up, and after a few hours of rest, we met to discuss how to recover the stolen horses. We didn't feel that Josey's boy would cause us any trouble so the marshal led us to the box canyon where we discovered two sets of fresh horse tracks coming out. We concluded the boy had not returned, but was hiding somewhere or watching us or his father.

We entered the box canyon. After a mile or so we came to a crude fence across a narrow part of the canyon. Beyond that a little valley opened up. The stolen horses were grazing peacefully.

There was a small spring bubbling from under a ledge on the south side of the canyon. There wasn't enough water to maintain a stream and it soon sank into the dry ground. It was a natural hideout.

We headed the horses towards the valley and drove them to the nearest ranch, where we left them for the ranchers to claim.

"Well, Mr. Hamblin," I said as we rode towards town. "Does that complete our mission?"

"For you, yes. I wish I could leave with you but I have to talk some sense into Josey or ask the marshal to keep him locked up until a trial can be held. I'd hate to see that happen now that we have all the horses back. You might as well go home."

The next morning I headed home, my thoughts turned from horse stealing to Laura, whom I knew would be eagerly awaiting my arrival.

Chapter XIV

About the first of October I received word from Marshal John Holden to meet him in Vernal. Our first child was due any time and I hated to leave. Laura was busy trying to preserve all the food she could for winter. Without many of the conveniences that she was used to, she was struggling. I knew Mother was helping her every day, but I still worried. Often I wondered if I should have stayed in the mines where she could have lived close to her folks.

When I reached Vernal, John was waiting for me.

"What's the trouble?" I asked.

"More cattle rustling," he replied.

"Jesse Challis?" I asked.

"The ranchers around here don't think so."

"Who do they think is doing it?" I asked.

"They think it's a young gang called the Wild Bunch."

"Who are they?"

"Young fellows from around the area mixed with a few drifters."

"Where did they take the cattle?"

"Towards the Green River. We'll follow their trail tomorrow."

That night John and I strolled around the small town.

Eventually we entered a saloon. To my great astonishment I heard my name called as I walked towards the bar. I looked around to see Roy sitting at a table playing cards.

"Wil," Roy repeated as he jumped up and started towards me. I met him part way. "What a wonderful surprise," he exclaimed, as we grasped hands.

"What are you doing way out here?" he asked.

"Doing a little investigating. I'm a deputy marshal now," I answered. "What are you doing here? When did you leave Marysvale?"

"Right after you did. I couldn't get along without you and Laura," he grinned. "How is she?"

"She's fine, I hope. We're expecting our first child soon. But what are you doing here in Vernal? Are you working on a cattle ranch?"

"No, just riding through. I got tired of the mines in Colorado. I guess I'm just looking for a little adventure."

"If you're heading home, I'm sure your parents will be glad to see you."

"I'd like to see them too. Maybe I'll ride that way and say hello one of these days."

"Are you married?" I asked. I was almost sure he wasn't. I never thought he could settle down that much.

"No, I'm too restless. Maybe later," he smiled as he looked at me. I invited him to go along with us the next day but he declined. I told him we were trying to run down some rustlers. He smiled and said he was glad I was doing so well.

We enjoyed a good visit that evening. It was great to see him again but he seemed evasive every time I asked about his work. I wondered if perhaps he was earning his keep by gambling.

I hated to see the evening come to an end but I had to be up early, so when John was ready to leave, I went with him.

"Please come see us, Roy. You know you're always welcome." He thanked me and said he'd try to do it but to be sure and tell Laura hello.

"Who was that?" John asked as we left the saloon.

"Roy Parker, one of the best friends I ever had. We bunked together when I was living in Marysvale. We worked in the mines together."

"Some believe he could be one of the rustlers," John said. "I'd heard the name but never met him."

"Roy, a rustler?" I said in complete astonishment. John said nothing more, but as we walked in the dark back to our camp the thought worried me.

The next morning we met the marshal and his posse and took up the rustlers' trail. They put me out in the lead and followed close behind. The tracks led east toward the Green River. Although they were nearly a week old, there had been no rain and the trail was easy to follow. As we rode along I kept thinking of Roy and what John had said.

We kept moving until we reached the river. There we found a few strays along the banks but most of the herd had been pushed across the river. The Colorado border wasn't far beyond so we knew there was little hope of overtaking the herd.

We rode up and down the stream for miles and decided the rustlers knew the terrain better than we did. They had probably used this same route before, and maybe would try it again. We also found that some of the rustlers' horses were shod and some were not, but that was not unusual. We felt sure the rustlers were not Indians.

While we were exploring the area we camped on the riverbank where there was plenty of feed for our horses. We concluded that if the cattlemen were more alert, maybe some future herds of stolen cattle could be intercepted because this had to be one of the main trails across the river.

On our way back to Vernal the marshal told us about a hideout near the south end of the San

Rafael swell, where many outlaws hid. He figured someday we would be forced to invade it.

The next morning I left early as I was very concerned about Laura. I pushed Blackie extra hard to get home as fast as I could. I wanted to be there when our first child was born.

The great event happened the second day after I arrived home. The new little boy was howling and kicking before Mother could get him bathed. I was so glad that Laura was all right for she was the dearest thing that had ever happened to me. My life had been hard, I thought, but she made it all bearable. I loved her so very much.

We named our new son Albert, after Laura's father.

As the months passed I was called on to help with different problems. As I thought about all the cattle rustling going on, I could never get Roy out of my mind. I couldn't believe that he would get involved in anything like rustling, yet whenever I stopped to see his folks, I always left feeling that something was worrying them. I remembered the evening in Vernal and his evasive answers. The gossip about him worried me.

More and more stories circulated about Butch Cassidy and the Wild Bunch. The two were always linked together as though there was a connection. I thought Roy was a leader but I still couldn't accept the idea that he was Butch Cassidy, the rustler and bank robber who led the Wild Bunch. It just didn't fit his character in my thinking.

I tried to ignore the gossip, hoping someday someone would capture Butch Cassidy and prove once and for all that Roy was not the outlaw. Sometimes Laura and I would talk about the stories we had heard. She didn't believe them any more than I did and it upset both of us to hear the accusations. We figured we had lived around him much longer than anybody, except his family, and knew his nature and disposition well enough to conclude he was not an outlaw. We had always found him to be generous and kind and willing to help people rather than hurt them. Often we talked about writing to Roy and asking him to visit us and clear up all the gossip, but we never did.

The next spring while I was riding on the mountain, I saw some Indians coming down the valley. As I watched I recognized one of them as my mining friend, Charley Dutson. They rode up to me and stopped.

"Hello, Wil," Charley said as he raised his hand in greeting.

"Hello, Charley," I said. "I thought you were still in the mines. When did you leave?"

"Last fall," Charley answered. "I got tired of being cooped up so much. Where are you living now, Wil?"

"We run a farm down the canyon to the east. We graze our cattle up here in the summer."

"We're headed for Grass Valley to catch some fish to dry. My people are hungry. They have been trying to get me to kill one of these cattle. Are any of them yours?"

"Yes," I answered.

"Will you sell us one?" he asked.

"No," I said, "but I'll give you one. Follow me."

We rode down along the stream where a half dozen animals were feeding. I circled around the bunch until I saw a two-year old steer with our brand on it.

Pointing to it I said, "Take that one, Charley. It belongs to me."

"Thanks my friend," he said. "If you need anything, let me know."

"Good luck to you and your people," I said as I continued on my ride up the valley to check on the other cattle, including those of my neighbors.

It seemed everything had been going well in our new settlement. Crops were planted, more fences were put up and new houses and sheds were built. The community kept growing slowly. Every year more land was put under cultivation.

The Indians and whites traded peacefully with each other most of the time. When Indian trouble did occur, I usually found that it was caused by some outlaw who had cheated the Indians or stolen something from them. With Charley Dutson's help, we worked to keep things under control. Twice we captured the outlaws by trailing them and surprising them when they thought they were safe.

In July a letter came from Leah asking Laura if we could come home for her wedding. She was going to marry Harry Dawson on the first day of August. Laura was excited and begged me to take her to the wedding.

I didn't like Harry and the way he treated Laura, but I couldn't say no to her request to go home to her sister's wedding, so we made preparations for the trip. We asked Nancy to go along and help us with Little Al and our new little girl, Laura Bell.

Three days before the big event, we started up the canyon, making fairly good time. Much work had been done on the dugway so travel was easier and faster.

We reached Marysvale the next day about noon. Laura was happy to be home. This was the first time she had visited her parents since we were married three years earlier. She walked through the house looking at all the familiar rooms and furniture.

The house looked like a palace compared to what we had. I hoped that perhaps someday, when we owned many cattle, we could build a bigger house and have beautiful chairs and tables too.

I was putting the team in the barn when I saw Harry and Leah go in the house to see Laura and the children. I was glad I had missed Harry. I could just see him bending over, kissing Laura's hand and her beaming from ear to ear at his gallantry. I knew I was jealous, but I also knew Harry overdid some things.

The wedding was a big social event in the small country community. Everyone was invited to the barbecue that followed. Some of Harry's friends were going to harass Harry and Leah, but the newly-weds slipped away during the celebration to a place that only Laura knew about.

The next morning, Mr. Bybe came out to help me harness my team.

"Wil, can Laura and the children stay with us for about ten days?" he asked. "We'd like to get better acquainted with the children. I'll bring them home. I've been wanting to see that part of the country. Maybe I'll buy a place down that way and put what cattle I have on it. Do you think that will be all right and will you help run my cattle?"

I was following along with him just fine until he suggested that Harry and Leah might want to come over to Tropic and live on the new place he wanted to get. He thought Harry could clear the land, build the fences, and help with the cattle. I nodded in agreement when he said he didn't know how hard Harry would work, or how responsible he would be.

I hesitated before speaking. I did not want Harry anywhere near Laura. But I knew Laura would be happy to have Leah around. Leah would be happy too. And Mr. Bybe was asking me for a favor.

"I'll look for a piece of ground," I promised. "There's a small valley a few miles east of us with water running through it that's partly open for homesteaders. I'll stake a place out for you."

The next morning I kissed Laura and the children goodbye and headed the team for home.

It was a little over a week later when Mr. Bybe drove in with his wife, Laura and the children. "Harry and Leah will be here tomorrow, probably," he said. "They are bringing a team and wagon and their belongings."

I told him about the farm I had staked out for him, and suggested we ride over there. I told him the new place needed lots of work, but that I thought the location was good.

Late that afternoon Mr. Bybe and I drove to the small valley. He liked what he saw and said he would file the papers to acquire the property as soon as he could.

I told him that if he wanted to bring his cattle down, Ned and Dad had promised to help take care of them. I told him to be sure and bring a branding iron with the cattle, that most of the branding took place after calving.

Because there was not a house on the new farm, Laura and her mother located a small one-room cabin toward the lower part of the town for Harry and Leah to live in until Harry built a new house on the homestead.

Everyone seemed happy with the arrangement. All but me. I didn't say anything to anyone but I still didn't want Harry around. Even though he had married Leah, I still didn't trust him around Laura.

That fall Mr. Bybe had his small herd of cattle trailed to the canebreaks area where we drove them into a canyon with some of ours for the winter. Although the summer heat dried up most of the feed, as soon as the fall storms began rolling in, the winter grass began growing, and the springs picked up too. It was a good place for the cattle in the winter and I never worried that they would starve down there. Our main worry was rustlers, so we tried to check the cattle often.

Chapter XV

The winter passed with the usual activities and work. All the settlers seemed to be building or improving what they had, all except Harry. He seemed content to lie around and rest. I stayed away from him, although Laura and Leah were constantly visiting each other. They were singing for church and social gatherings, and were very popular.

My work often took me out of town. When I was gone, I always asked Ned to help Laura with the chores because I didn't want Harry around.

When spring came we moved the cattle to their summer range. Soon after, I rode up on the mountain to check them. While I was up there I decided to ride up the eastern side of the plateau through the big pines to check the grazing possibilities.

Upon reaching the stream I noticed a cloud of dust further down the valley. Then I saw two riders moving some cattle at a fast pace. I didn't like what I saw and decided to check it out. I thought it best to keep out of sight, carefully following the trail, trying to stay in the cover of the trees wherever possible. The trail led over the low foothills toward the west for about three miles. I followed slowly until I couldn't see any more dust, and could hear cattle.

I dismounted under a shady tree, tied Blackie and slipped up to the next rise. I saw what I believed were some of our cattle on the lower edge of a large herd. I studied them through my field glasses. I could see our brand plus those belonging to some of my neighbors.

A lone rider was just beyond the herd. Four other men were standing by a chuck wagon. It looked as if one of them was paying some money to the others.

I thought of Roy and what I had heard about him. He was not among the men. Many of the ranchers in the area were Roy's friends and I was sure he wouldn't steal from his friends even if he were rustling. No, the leader of this band of rustlers had to be Jesse Challis.

Just then I saw dust coming from the west. As I waited I saw two riders hurrying a small bunch of cattle toward the herd. I concluded they must be stealing cattle from all directions.

If only I had some help. Even with a badge I felt uneasy about trying to handle the situation alone.

As I lay there pondering what to do, a plan formed in my mind. I decided that after it got dark and the riders were asleep or on the other side of the herd, I'd slip in and recover our cattle. Jesse Challis was stealing from us, so I would steal from him. I was sure he was behind all of this.

I hoped Jesse wouldn't even discover the missing cattle. But even if he did, I didn't think he would dare do anything.

I smiled as I thought about how I was going to get even, just a little, with that thief. Someday I hoped I would catch him fair and square and send him to jail. In the meantime, I could just rustle from the rustler.

After it was dark and the fire had burned low, I stood up and patted Blackie on the neck, whispering for him to be quiet, then led him around the point of the hill. Quietly, I rode among the cattle I planned to recover and moved slowly away with them. As soon as I was a good distance away and I could hear no one in pursuit, I moved them faster. We reached the stream and started up the valley.

I thought of leaving the cattle in the trees but decided to take them down to the holding corral where I could show the people the evidence in case it was needed.

Morning was almost breaking when I reached home. Quietly, I stretched out on the couch and went to sleep. Laura found me there when she arose. As she was fixing breakfast I told her how I had fooled Jesse Challis.

After chores were completed I laid back down to nap again.

About eleven o'clock Marshal Cope came to the house and asked for me. Laura woke me up.

I went to the door to greet the marshal.

"I hate to ask you this, Wil," he began, a serious look on his face. "We have a problem. Were you up on the mountain yesterday?"

"Yes, I was."

"Did you drive any cattle down to the holding corral?"

"Yes, I did. Why?"

"A Mr. Challis says someone stole some cattle from him and he tracked them to the holding corral. The cattle in there have your brand, some of the neighbors brands, and there are three with a Lazy C on the right side. He says they are his, and they are stolen."

My smile changed to an audible groan. I was so sure of myself and thought I had pulled one on Challis. In my hurry to get down the mountain, I hadn't noticed that three head carried the Challis brand. I knew Challis would press charges. Witnesses had seen his cattle in my corral, and I had no bill of sale to show they were mine. I had been caught rustling cattle.

We rode out to the corral. I saw my own cattle, those of my neighbors and the three others.

Challis was standing beside the corral. He smiled when he saw me. He knew that if I confessed to bringing his cattle in, he had me cold. He could prove by the trail that they came from his herd.

"Wil says he drove them down last night but he didn't know some of yours were among those he brought in," the marshal said.

"That is only a ruse to protect his thievery," Challis growled. "He ought to be strung up like the rest of the cattle rustlers."

"Someday I'll get even with you," I promised.

"Don't do anything foolish, Wil," the marshal said. Then turning to Challis he said. "Take the three that have your brand on them and leave."

"I want them all. I bought them."

"If you want to take the chance of being arrested for possessing stolen property then take them, but these men say they have not sold any so I suggest you think real good before you do."

Challis grumbled as he turned and told his companion to cut the three out from the bunch and start up the trail.

"When I go through Marysvale, I'll contact the judge to see when the trial will be held so I can be there for the hearing," he snarled. Then he left, his snarl turning to a smile.

I told the marshal and the other men what happened the day before.

"I thought I was just getting even with that crook," I said.

"I'm sorry Wil," the marshal said. "Challis will push this to the limit. I'll contact the judge and see when the hearing will be held. We can explain it all to him and see if he can dismiss the case." The marshal mounted his horse. I looked up at him.

"I don't think Challis will let that happen," I said. "He knows I'm a threat to him and his operation. He'll push this as far as he can."

"I'll let you know as soon as I hear anything," the marshal said as he rode away.

My family and Laura were upset at what had happened. Laura sat down and wrote a letter to her father asking him to help. She sent it out by the first mail.

A few days later John Holden rode into town. I told him the whole story.

"I sympathize with you," John said, "but I don't think you can beat it. I guess Challis buys enough to cover up his stealing. We'll get him one of these days. If you do get locked up for awhile, I'll go to bat for you when you get out. We need you and next time don't let some creep like Challis frame you. He probably mixed those cattle hoping you would do just what you did. See you later."

After having said his piece he just rode away. Up until John dropped in I had a hard time believing I might really go to jail. Now I was worried.

I worked around the farm until the next week when I was told to appear at the hearing. We drove to Marysvale where Mr. Bybe was waiting to act as my lawyer. Challis was there too.

When I went before the judge, Challis' lawyer insisted I go to jail. He argued that many cattle thieves were hung for less than what I had done.

Eventually I was sentenced to three years in the territorial prison in Sugarhouse, near Salt Lake City.

"If Challis and his cronies had stayed away I think we could have won," Mr. Bybe said. "I'm sorry, Wil. We'll see that Laura and the children are taken care of. They can come and live with us. I would like to have little Al and Belle around and so would Mother."

After the sentence was pronounced, Laura came over to me. I put my arms around her as we both shed tears. I loved her so much and I hated Challis just as strongly. I swore vengeance on that thief.

I made up my mind that I would serve my term and return for two main reasons. First to be with my family and loved ones and second to trap that crook. I had underestimated him this time, but never again. He had been rustling cattle for years and knew all the tricks. I knew I would have plenty of time to plan my strategy while sitting in jail.

My greatest worry now was Laura and the children. I found comfort in knowing the Bybe's would take good care of them. I also worried how I was going to endure without them. I couldn't believe the mess I was in and it was all Jesse Challis' fault.

The judge charged John Holden with delivering me to the territorial prison near Salt Lake City. After a few minutes with my family, John came over to me. He touched my arm and motioned for me to follow him.

He never made any move to handcuff me, but he did stop and look at me.

"Wil, I have always trusted you and still do. Is there any reason to use these?" he asked as he pointed to the handcuffs.

"None at this moment," I replied, "although I don't relish the thought of being locked up in jail."

"If you can keep busy it won't be so bad and I don't think they will keep you there very long," he said as we headed for the livery stable.

A week later when the warden read my file he called me into his office. "I have talked to John Holden and I have just read your history. I'll say right now that I believe you were framed about as cleverly as any man could be. If you'll behave I'll make you a trustee. Where would you like to work?"

"I get along best with animals. I can trust them," I answered.

"All right, the barns and stables then. We have some good stock and I know you'll like the riding horses."

I was taken back to my cell where I asked for paper and pen so I could write to Laura.

My Darling Laura,

How I miss you and the children. This is such an undesirable place to be in. I have to pinch myself to be sure it is not all a bad dream. How did I ever get into this situation, anyway? I was only trying to do what was fair and right. I guess I was too naive to deal with such crooks. Well, I learned my lesson and I'll show those characters when I get out that I can be just as hard as they can be. Challis is the ring leader and John Holden says he'll get him. If he doesn't, I will.

Tell your father thanks for all he did to help me. Maybe I can pay him back some day.

Kiss the children for me and take good care of yourself.

I love you, Wil

Laura stayed with her parents the rest of the summer. She wanted to go home for the winter because it was much warmer in Tropic, and she said she missed Leah and her little home. I didn't blame her, though I preferred that she stay in Marysvale, away from Harry.

That winter, Father, Mother, along with Ned and my two sisters, took good care of Laura and the children. Laura lived in our home but spent much time with my folks and Leah. She kept the milk cow, along with the chickens. I knew Ned would keep the wood box filled.

Very little help was received from Harry. When Laura was around I knew he would be very attentive, but working beyond his own needs was too much. He hadn't even started the house on the farm yet. He always said, later.

The time passed slowly for Laura. She started singing again with Leah and often stayed at her house. Leah was expecting a child in May so Laura helped her the best she could. But their little one-room house was so small that not much could be done but cook and wash dishes.

Harry milked the cow most of the time and chopped most of the wood. He didn't always bring it in the house so Laura helped Leah do that. The thought that Laura might stay with Leah really worried me.

"I want to go home to have the baby," Leah told Laura one evening. Since the baby was due in May, they decided not to take any more singing engagements.

"When do you want to leave?" asked Laura.

"The first of May comes next week so I have asked Harry to drive me down next Tuesday. I hate to leave you alone that long but we'll be back within a month, I think."

"What does Harry think about it?" Laura asked.

"He says it's fine with him, that it will give him a chance to visit his friends," Leah replied.

136

"I'll come over Monday evening and help you pack your clothes," volunteered Laura.

Harry drove Leah to Marysvale as they had planned. He had a chance to visit his old haunts and brag about his new ranch and the cattle he was going to raise.

The days dragged by slowly.

"I'm going back to the ranch," Harry announced one morning.

"You haven't even been here a week. I thought that you were going to stay here and help," Leah said.

"I'm not doing anybody any good here and I could be working on the place if I went home."

"I want to start the plowing," he continued. "You let me know as soon as the baby is born and the day that you want me to pick you up and I'll be back."

"You know I won't be able to travel with the baby for weeks so why don't you stay here?" reasoned Leah.

Harry offered no further arguments. He just packed his things and left.

Chapter XVI

Two days later Harry reached home. He turned the horses loose in the field, gathered the eggs and walked over to Laura's.

"Hello, Laura. How's my beautiful sister-in-law?"

"Come in, Harry. I know you're flattering me but it sounds good anyway. Even married women appreciate a compliment once in a while."

"Complimenting you is easy, because it's the truth." He handed her a bucket of eggs.

"Thanks. We can always use more," she said. "But when did you get back, and how is Leah? I thought you were going to stay with her?"

"I stayed most of a week and things were getting boring," Harry replied.

"Sit down and stay for supper. I'll get the rest of the chores done and then we can eat. You can tell me all about who you saw and what's going on. I haven't heard much since Wil left."

"Let me finish the chores while you fix the meal," Harry offered.

"The pigs and the chickens need to be fed and the cow hasn't been milked," Laura said.

Soon Harry was finished and they sat down with the two children to eat. Harry told Laura about the people he had seen and what was going on in Marysvale.

The more Harry talked about Laura's old friends and what was happening, the more she realized what she was missing.

"I wish I had gone with you and Leah," she said. "I could have visited with Mother and Dad, at least. Maybe I should have stayed with them last fall, but I felt it best to come home and wait."

"I'll bet you've been lonesome and homesick here alone with only the children to talk to," Harry volunteered.

"Wil's family is close and then I've had you and Leah, but it surely isn't the same. Yes, I get awfully lonesome," she replied.

"You won't have to be alone so much now that I'm back. I'll come over every night and do the chores," Harry promised. He told her what a good cook she was when he had finished eating the food on his plate.

"Give Leah time. She'll be just as good," Laura said.

"Well, good night," Harry said as he started for the doorway. "I'll see you tomorrow."

She knew Harry had been flattering her. Still it had made her feel good. Harry's words had helped her forget some of her loneliness. She thought about what he had said as she cleaned up the dishes and put the children to bed.

The next evening about sundown, Harry knocked on the door, then entered before Laura had a chance to open it. He was pleased to see her in one of her best dresses. There was a ribbon in her hair. Harry paused.

"Beautiful," he gasped. "I always thought you were one of the most beautiful women around."

"You are a soft-soaper, Harry. But it's always nice to hear compliments anyway," Laura responded.

"After supper when the children are in bed, I'll take you outside and show you a beautiful full moon," promised Harry. "We can sit on the porch and watch it climb over the trees."

"Where is the milk bucket and I'll get started," Harry said, eagerly.

After supper, in spite of their protesting, the children were put right to bed. Harry and Laura walked out and sat on the porch. The moon was clear and full.

For a brief moment, Laura hesitated. She knew she shouldn't be alone like this with Harry. She was still married to Wil, and Harry was her sister's husband. On the other hand she hadn't felt so alive, so happy in months. Harry's words were like medicine to her aching heart. When he placed his arm around her waist she slowly pushed it away.

"I have never seen anything more beautiful than Laura in the moonlight," he said, pulling her close to him. "Your loveliness is too much to resist."

"Harry, this isn't right," she whispered, suddenly realizing she must resist his advances, before it was too late. She removed his arm and scooted to the far end of the bench. "You've always been a romantic suitor," she said, her voice tense.

"Don't hold back," he said, his voice calm and soothing. "You're lonesome, and so am I. It isn't natural to push love away. You know I've always wanted you."

"Wil's gone now," he continued, sliding closer to her. "No one knows when he will be back. I love you, Laura."

"Please don't say that, Harry," she begged. "What about Leah? She loves you. Don't you love her?"

"I love her, and I love you too." he exclaimed. "We're here; our mates are far away and we don't know for sure when they'll be coming back. We can't let life and love slip away. Besides a little love won't hurt anyone," he said as he put his arms around her and kissed her.

Laura started to pull away, then relaxed. It felt so nice just to be next to someone.

"That's enough, Harry. Good night," she said, pushing away from him and standing up. Without another word she hurried in the cabin, closing the door firmly behind her.

The next night Harry was back, and every night after that. He usually brought eggs with him, helped milk the cow, and usually stayed for supper. Mary and the girls always visited Laura and the children during the middle of the day so they didn't know that Harry was back. Ned went over one evening to see if Laura had enough wood chopped and saw Harry milking the cow. He cut and stacked a pile of wood and returned home. That night he told his parents about finding Harry at Laura's.

"I wonder how long he's been back?" Mary said, thoughtfully. "I wish he wouldn't hang around there when Wil isn't home. I never did like that man. I don't trust him."

Harry and Laura began spending their evenings on the porch, in the moonlight. Harry's smooth, flattering manner was wearing Laura's resistance down. She was lonely and Harry made her feel good.

Mary worried about what was happening, but she didn't dare say anything. She felt sorry for Laura, and wished Leah would send word for Harry to come after her. Mary hoped everything would be all right once the baby was born. One evening she discussed the situation with her husband.

"We must trust them," Hyrum said. "At least I trust Laura."

"But I don't trust that Harry," Mary exclaimed. "If anything happened, I don't know what Wil would do. He loves Laura so much."

One day Laura received a letter telling her that Leah had a new blue-eyed, blond girl. Leah named her Harriet after her father. Harry was supposed to come after them in a few weeks.

At the time I didn't know any of this was going on. I was lonesome too, and spent my time with the animals. They seemed to stabilize me and take my mind off the desire to run away.

I was always hungry for word from my family. Laura's letters were not coming as regularly as they once had. I worried that something might be wrong. I had an uneasy feeling whenever I thought about Laura being home alone.

Eventually one year had passed and the warden told me that in a few months he would recommend a parole if I kept up the good work. I was a trusted prisoner but sometimes the urge to escape was so strong I could hardly resist doing something about it. During those times I would work long hours around the riding horses.

I often dreamed of the open range and freedom. The hardest thing I had to contend with was the desire to hurry to my beloved Laura and my children.

The hatred I held for Jesse Challis kept me
thinking up ways to catch the crook.

Chapter XVII

My second Christmas brought a letter and a small gift from home. The letters from Mother seemed to be guarded, as did Laura's. The feeling that something was wrong kept coming back. Finally a plea to Laura to please tell me if there was any trouble, brought a heart-rending reply.

My Dear Wil,

First let me say that I love you very much. When you get out, please hurry home. I need you and so do the children. They often ask about you and when you will come home.

I am so glad to hear that you might be paroled this coming summer. Please don't spoil the chance.

I don't know how to tell you this and I am surprised that you haven't heard before, but I guess it's up to me to tell you the bad news. I believe I would rather die than write this. I am expecting a baby in February.

If you don't read past this part I won't blame you.

It happened when Leah was in Marysvale with her new baby. Harry decided to come back home to wait. We were both lonesome. I guess I let him get a little closer than I should have, but I didn't think anything like this could happen. Because he is Leah's husband it never occurred to me that he would force himself upon me. I trusted him more than I should have.

God bless you and remember I will always love you.

Your repentant Laura

I stumbled to the horse barns, already making plans how I would kill that worthless, conniving Harry. Maybe Laura was lonesome, but I didn't blame her, only Harry. He had wanted Laura ever since I had met him, and he finally figured out a way to get her. The dirty, loathsome, scum of the earth. "He doesn't deserve to live," I thought. I promised myself that I'd really kill him.

In the following weeks I spent so much extra time at the barns that the guards were suspicious that I was planning a break. They told the warden and he called me to his office.

"Wil, everything has gone well so far and I was going to recommend you for a parole this August," he said. "Don't let anything ruin it."

I said nothing.

The warden continued. "The guards say something is bothering you. Do you want to talk about it?"

"Not now," I finally said.

"Maybe I could help," he said.

"I don't think so," I said. "But don't worry. I will not try to escape."

I didn't want to say anything, fearing the Warden might guess what I intended to do to Harry, and delay the parole plans. I decided not to discuss the situation with anyone until I got out. Then I'd give that skunk, Harry, a chance to leave the country or take the consequences.

The hatred inside boiled and seethed incessantly. Every hour of every day the anger pounded in my skull. I worked like a man possessed. Everyone saw the change and knew it had something to do with that letter I had received from home. They said little, but watched me continually, wondering what I might do.

On the first of August I received my parole. The warden wished me good luck and admonished me to be careful and not let another impulsive act spoil my life. He was very concerned about my changed disposition, but since I wouldn't confide in him he didn't know how to counsel me. He was just worried and concerned. I thanked him and left.

Although the railroad had made its way into the Utah Territory by this time, there was no route south so I caught rides as best I could.

When I reached Marysvale I stopped at the Bybes. I'm sure they were wondering if I knew about Laura's new baby girl, but nobody said anything, at least not at first.

"What are your plans, Wil?" Mr. Bybe asked.

"I don't have many but what I do have are definite," I responded, cheerfully. "First I'm going to kill Harry Dawson, then go back to prison or be hung, probably. After that I don't know."

"Do you think killing Harry will solve anything?" he asked.

"Yes," I said. "Harry has never done anything useful in his whole life. All he's ever done was take from somebody else. It's time someone put a stop to it."

"Have you thought that maybe it was partly Laura's fault?"

"I don't believe that for one second. You could probably say it was partly my fault too, for not being around. But you know Harry. All he ever needed was an excuse and someone's guard down for a few minutes."

"Think about Leah and her baby," Mr. Bybe pleaded.

"I have. She was probably fooled by Harry's smooth ways and gushy manners just like most everyone else. You know he'll try it again and with some other man's wife. Maybe I'll just castrate him instead of kill him."

Mr. Bybe looked around the room trying to decide what he could say that would make a difference. "Wil, I've admired you ever since Laura brought you home that first time. You're a hard worker. You've always been responsible and treated people with concern. But there's too much hate in you, Wil. Please don't let it destroy all the good you've done."

"Will you loan me a horse?" I asked. "I'll get him back to you as soon as I can."

"Sure, take your pick," he said, knowing the conversation was going nowhere. Then he handed me a letter to take to Laura.

Mr. Bybe told me he had been worrying about what I might do to Laura but now he was sure she would be safe. He said the note to Laura included a message to Harry to get away as quickly as he could. He said he wasn't pleased with Harry any more than I was. He just didn't want me to go back to jail, leaving Laura alone again. Even more than that he said he didn't want to see me hang.

Soon my horse was saddled and ready to leave. I led him out to the front of the house. Laura's mother handed me a second sealed letter and said, "Give my love to the girls and the children. I wish we lived closer. Good luck, Wil. I hope things work out the best for all concerned. And, Wil, remember Albert and I greatly admire you and your goodness to Laura. We know you want the best for her and

149

will work hard to see that she gets it. Bring them over to see us soon."

"Thanks," I said as I rode away. Everyone seemed so happy and pleasant at my departure that I wondered it they took my threat seriously. I guessed not. Maybe that was for the best.

I rode all day, reaching my parents' cabin late that night. They heard me come in and got up to see who it was.

"Oh, Wil! Wil!," Mother said as she threw her arms around me. "Why didn't you let us know you were coming?"

"I wanted to surprise you," I answered. "How is everyone?"

"We're fine, but you look so thin," she said in the dim light.

I assured her I was fine, then surprised the family by asking to spend the night.

"You know you can stay here anytime you want," she said, obviously puzzled, wondering why a man who had just spent 18 months in prison did not want to be with his wife.

Mother watched me as I shook hands with Father and Ned and hugged my sisters. I knew she was wondering how much I knew, and what I might do.

I handed Mother the letters to Laura, asking her to give them to Laura in the morning. I said I wanted to ride up to the farm early and look at the crops and stock.

"Sure," she replied. She wanted to talk to me longer but I walked into Ned's room to go to bed and closed the door behind me. I left them all standing there with many unanswered questions.

I'm sure as they went back to bed Mother and Father were wondering what I was really going to do the next day.

A full moon was shining through the window. Quickly, I undressed and stretched out on the extra cot in the far corner of the room. I knew Ned always slept in the one near the door.

Although I had ridden all night, I couldn't fall asleep. I heard Ned's deep breathing. I guess all the hurt and anger of the last few months were come more into focus. Being so close to home and Laura and Harry seemed to intensify everything. My longing and love for Laura only made by pain more excruciating.

After a couple of hours of rolling and tossing I dressed quietly, and carrying my shoes in my hand, slipped through the door and moved towards the peg where I had seen my .44 hanging a few hours before. Lifting the gun belt I slipped it over my arm.

I remembered where Mother used to keep the jerky so I opened the lower cupboard door and reached into the big crock jar. Sure enough, the dried meat was still there. I grabbed a handful. Jerky had always been a favorite of mine and I knew it would sustain me for days.

I stepped out the back door and closed it carefully behind me. After putting my shoes on I headed for the stable where the big sorrel was waiting. I knew he was tired, but I intended to go only a short distance. Then he could eat and rest for hours while we waited to see if Harry would leave the country.

I saddled the horse and led him to the gate that led up the lane toward the box canyons.

In less than an hour we reached the breaks. They were still as beautiful as I remembered them, and just as rough and rugged.

When I reached the mountain stream that came from the south, I crossed it and started riding parallel to it. I remembered that two or three of the box canyons had small springs in them. I headed up the first one. As we moved between the tall, narrow ledges I could reach out and almost touch both sides at the same time. It was still night as we moved between the walls. The moon that had enabled me to see the canyon walls from the outside was now blocked out.

After a short distance, the canyon opened up where the moonlight flooded a round, small basin. At the foot of a big ledge gurgled a small spring. Grass grew all along the bank and I knew my horse would have plenty to eat and drink.

I dismounted and removed the saddle. Taking a pair of hobbles from the saddlebags, I put them on the horse's front feet and then removed the bridle. He looked at me and then at the clear small stream.

"Help yourself," I said as I patted his neck. "Just stay close by." He reached down and drank deeply then started cropping the tender, untouched grass.

I placed the saddle under a small pine tree that grew all alone near the spring. It would produce some welcome shade during the hot day.

I knew we were alone. I rested my head on the saddle and looked up at the fading morning stars. It was peaceful there and my fatigue became too much for the anger in my heart. As I looked at those familiar stars, I decided to give Harry, plenty of time to escape. I would give him until the next day. Down deep in my heart I hoped, yes, even prayed that he would leave.

Weariness finally got the best of me. I fell asleep, listening to the peaceful sound of the feeding horse.

When I awoke it was morning. The ghostly shadows and figures were fading fast. My horse was still eating and seemed content. Very little air stirred. I knew it was going to be a hot day.

I spent my day whittling a baby in a cradle out of a piece of dead tree root. It actually looked pretty good, I thought. The day dragged by slowly. The heat was terrible but I stayed in the shade of the little tree and rested. When evening finally came. I tucked the baby in my pocket and pulled my coat and the saddle blanket over me and went to sleep while my horse continued to graze and the coyotes howled their nightly songs.

By the next morning the big sorrel and I were both ready to move out. I hated to leave such a peaceful spot, but my business was urgent and unavoidable.

Chapter XVIII

When Mother arose the next morning after my arrival and discovered that I had left the house, she sent Nancy to Laura's with my letters. When Laura found out that I was back and had left without coming to see her and the children, she started to cry.

She opened the first letter and tried to read it, the tears rolling down her cheeks. The note from her father, telling her to warn Harry, seemed to take all the strength from her legs and she sank into a chair in despair. The worst thing in the world would be for Wil to go back to jail, or even worse, be hung. Finally, she asked Nancy to stay with the children while she ran over to Leah's.

Filled with new resolve, Laura ran most of the way. She burst through the door without knocking.

"Harry, where are you?" she demanded.

"What's wrong?" Harry asked, sitting up in bed. Leah was beside him.

"Wil came home last night but he stayed at his parents' home. He brought these letters from Mother with him."

"Where is he now?" Harry asked while Leah was reading one of the letters.

"Nancy said he stayed with them last night and then rode up the canyon to the farm early this morning. Dad must have been worried or he wouldn't have added that note. Harry you must get out of here. There's been too much trouble and heartache already."

Harry put his clothes on and then sat down in a chair.

"Hurry up, Harry. You must go, please. You know how Wil is. If he decides he'll do something, you know he'll do it, right or wrong," Laura insisted.

"I'm not leaving," Harry replied, stubbornly.

"If you stay here, he might kill you," Laura sobbed. I don't want Wil back in jail. Please, please, Harry, just give us a few days to work things out."

"You know how good a tracker Wil is," Harry reasoned. "If he's determined to find me, he will do just that. No, I'll arm myself and stay right here."

Harry went over to his gun which was hanging on the wall, took it out of the holster, checked the cylinder and loaded it. Then he sat down at the table facing the door.

"Oh, you stubborn men. You're all alike," Laura cried as she stalked out of the house. She hurried home to get breakfast for the children.

She thanked Nancy for watching the children, then asked her to hurry home and send her father back. Laura needed his help.

In about ten minutes, Hyrum appeared at the door wanting to know what was wrong.

Laura handed him the letter from her father and told him how she had tried to get Harry to leave town and how he had refused.

"Oh, Father Halladay, I love Wil and I don't want him back in prison. Won't you please find him and try to stop him. If I could only talk to him, maybe I could reason with him. Will you please help?"

"I'll ride up to the farm and see if I can find him," Hyrum offered.

Father rode to the farm and through all the neighboring hills but could not find me. He didn't know I had gone up into the breaks, hoping to give Harry a chance to leave. I didn't need to kill Harry, I just needed to be rid of him.

Laura stayed close to home all day hoping I would come back.

Harry paced back and forth in the little house, his gun in his hand, waiting for something to happen. When darkness came he would not go to bed. He didn't dare sleep for fear I would come during the night to keep my promise.

There wasn't much sleep for Leah that night either and I'm sure my family was trying to figure out a way to stop me. Only Harry could do that, by leaving.

On the morning of the second day Laura took the children to my mother's, so she could visit Harry again and try to talk some sense into him. At the same time I was riding out of the breaks to see what Harry had decided to do. He had had enough time.

Laura arrived ahead of me. She and Leah argued and talked to Harry until they were talked out, but Harry kept insisting that Wil was only bluffing and really didn't mean what he had said.

Laura tried to convince him that he should leave, if only for a week or two. Wil needed some time to cool down.

Finally, Harry stretched out on the bed for a nap. He hadn't slept all night, and was tired. Before going to sleep he cautioned Leah and Laura not to holler, "Come in", if someone knocked, but to see who it was.

Harry's gun was at his side as he began to snore.

Laura and Leah were sitting at the table trying to figure out what to do when I knocked. "Come in," Leah called without remembering what Harry had told her.

I opened the door and looked in. The women gasped. Harry sat up, grabbed his gun and fired at me, nicking my right ear. I could see him cocking back the hammer for a second shot. Everything seemed to move in slow motion. Wouldn't it be nice, I thought, if we could just kill each other? I fired and Harry fell back on the bed.

"Wil, stop," Laura screamed. We stood there looking at each other as Leah ran to Harry.

"I think he's dead," Leah sobbed.

I didn't have to think. I could see the blood oozing out of the left side of Harry's vest. Harry's eyes slowly lost their focus as his muscles relaxed. Harry was dead alright.

"Why did you have to do it?" cried Laura. "You might as well shoot me, too. You'll go back to prison and I'll have nothing to live for. We could have started over. Now look what you've done. I might as well be dead too."

My heart ached to take her in my arms, but I did nothing. I was numb all over. There were tears streaming down the faces of the two women, but my eyes were dry. Time seemed to be standing still. It hadn't even felt good to kill Harry.

The sounds of the shots brought the neighbors and the marshal on the run. Leah's frantic efforts to revive Harry were fruitless. She collapsed across his chest sobbing. It had never occurred to me that she might really love Harry. How could anyone love Harry?

The noise in the yard startled me enough that my legs began to work. I turned and walked out to the gate to meet the marshal. As I handed the gun to him I said, "I've just killed a snake." I held out my hands so the marshal could handcuff me. We walked away.

Leaning back against the wall, Laura slowly sank to the floor in the corner of the kitchen. "How can I go on living?" she moaned, certain that everything that had happened was her fault. "I didn't mean to. I told him no. I didn't want to."

Leah's sobs and the baby's crying brought Laura back to reality. She put her arms around Leah and slowly led her outside. They started towards Laura's house. There were others to think about. Others who needed her. She'd have to work through her feelings another day. A neighbor followed with the baby.

Not long after the funeral I was taken to Marysvale for the trial. Ned brought Laura, Leah and the children. Mr. Bybe represented me. The trial did not last long because I would not allow any plea but guilty. I was really sorry for the trouble I had caused, though I didn't feel very bad about Harry being gone.

The judge sentenced me to life in prison with a possible early parole for good behavior.

As John Holden led me from the courtroom, I was allowed to stop and give Albert and Laura Belle a hug. "Be good and mind your mother and be kind to her," I said. "She needs your help."

As I stood up I saw Laura standing nearby, tears rolling down her cheeks. My heart ached for her and a chance to hold her in my arms. Eighteen months in prison and five days out and I hadn't even touched her. But I wasn't sure she would ever allow that again.

I longed for the days when our love for each other was totally fulfilling, with nothing to hold us apart. I still loved her so very much but how could I make her understand that and believe it, now.

As I turned to leave, Laura spoke. I paused. I didn't dare look back. I never could stand to see her cry. It seemed as if my heart would break. Her tears seemed to melt me.

She came up to me, put her arms around me and through sobs, cried, "I just can't stand to see you leave this way. I love you so very much."

I lifted the handcuffs over her head and let my arms slid slowly down her shoulders and around her waist. "I have always loved you," I told her. "And I've longed for the day when I could return to you. My hatred has ruined it all." I hugged her tight and kissed her.

"Goodbye," I said. "Try to forget me. It isn't fair to keep you waiting forever."

"I'll be waiting, Wil." Laura sobbed as I left the room with Marshal Holden.

Elizabeth walked over to Laura and put her arms around the heaving shoulders and led her out the door towards home.

"Oh, Mother. What have I done?"

That night was a miserable, sleepless one for all of us. I knew I was lucky to escape hanging. If Harry hadn't shot first, I probably would have been sentenced to death.

What really worried me was Laura and the children. Although my family would help her, I knew she was independent and didn't always ask for help when she needed it. I almost wished that she would stay with her parents, but I was quite sure she would return home.

Leah was the one who stayed in Marysvale to live with her parents. Laura returned to our farm. Mother told me in a letter that Laura was milking the cow, taking care of the chickens and pigs and working hard in the garden.

She was still a pretty, young woman and could easily marry someone else if she chose to divorce me. It hurt to think about her doing something like that, but I figured there was nothing I could do about it one way or the other. All I could do was bury myself in my work and pray.

Why hadn't things been so clear before I killed Harry Dawson? Now I could see what I had done. I could see the long shadows of my actions reaching far into the lives of all who loved me. I could see now how I had literally deserted Laura when she needed me most. I had left my children unprotected and uncared for. My dreams of a large cattle ranch were gone. I had brought heartache and sorrow to my parents and Ned and Nancy and Ellen. Why couldn't I see it before?

Laura kept writing to me and encouraging me to do my best and hurry back to them as soon as I could. To me, going home seemed a million years away. I wasn't sure I would ever get out again, but she seemed certain it would happen and promised to wait.

Laura refused to sing for anything or anyone for almost two years. Finally her grief and embarrassment faded to the point that she thought it was time to get on with her life. The children were growing and needed to be involved in the church and community.

My family helped Laura and the children all the time.

Little Al spent much of his time with my father, tagging along every time he got a chance. He loved to ride Pete whenever Ned or Dad would put a saddle on the old horse. One thing they wouldn't let him do was miss school.

The girls spent a lot of time with my sisters and mother. They worked together, and that pleased me.

Each summer a number of cattle were driven off by rustlers. Jesse Challis was the number one suspect, but no one could trap him. Dad said John Holden came by once in a while but never told them much. They figured he was after Challis but they never knew for sure. Laura told me that whenever John stopped, he always asked about me. He told her that when I got out, he wanted me back on the force. I appreciated his kindness.

Laura worked hard, doing the daily chores, planting and weeding the garden. In the fall she bottled some of everything in the garden and orchard. She told me that the little fruit trees were producing more fruit every year. I knew Father and Ned would keep meat on the table.

They said everything was moving along rather smoothly except for the cattle rustling. It was impossible to build a herd with someone always stealing from it.

One day a new family moved into the community. They had a girl Ned's age. The two became good friends and I guess everyone figured they would eventually get married.

Ned had been hired by Mr. Bybe to take care of his cattle and the farm in the East Valley. Of course there wasn't much gain with the cattle because of the constant losses. At first Ned wondered if he should build a house on the Bybe farm but as he was helping Dad much of the time he decided he would buy a lot in town and build a house there.

I was happy they were doing as well as they were. I felt that if the rustling could be stopped, life would be better for everyone. I dreamed of getting out and going after Challis myself. Many nights I stayed awake planning how I would do it. I planned his capture a hundred times right down to the smallest detail. It felt good to have my mind busy.

When I returned to prison I was called into the warden's office. He sat and looked at me for what seemed a long time. Finally he spoke. "Do you want to talk about what happened?" he asked.

"There's not much to say," I shrugged. "What's done is done. Maybe there was a better solution than the one I came up with, but I sure couldn't think of anything else at the time."

"I wish you had talked it over with me before you left. I could have helped, Wil."

"Can I go back to the barns?" I asked.

"I doubt the board will agree to let you have that much freedom at first. I'll do what I can."

I was taken back and locked up. I hated those small cages. I made up my mind to be a model prisoner and get out as soon as possible.

It wasn't many days after that when a guard came to tell me that I was needed at the stock barns. The prison had bought a new saddle horse that was fighting everyone who tried to handle him.

It took me only a few days to have that beautiful bay gelding eating out of my hand. I called him Pacer because he was the one who rescued me from pacing back and forth in the small cell. I spent countless hours training Pacer until he seemed to understand every word I said. At the sight of me he

165

would come to me and follow me around while I did my other chores. With constant riding I was able to push him into a smooth rocking-chair-pace gait, between a walk and a trot. Developing this gait made the horse much more valuable in a day when people rode horses nearly everywhere they went.

Being sent to the barns to work with Pacer was the break I needed. I made up my mind that I would be careful, obey all rules and regulations and stay with the stock detail as long as they would let me.

The months dragged slowly along for all of us. On the second Christmas day after I returned to prison, Ned brought his girlfriend, Clara Hobson, home for Christmas dinner. She was a little taller than Laura with blue eyes and light brown hair. Ned was fairly tall with blue eyes and light brown hair, too. They were a good looking couple. It was about one o'clock when they walked in the house, just in time for the big dinner.

The dinner was delicious. A good beef roast, bottled vegetables and fruit and a big chocolate cake that Laura had made.

Laura was pleasant but silent. Mother knew she was thinking about me. They were both worrying and wondering what I was doing on that Christmas day.

Mother looked at Laura and as their gaze met, she saw tears. They both understood each other.

Mother never blamed Laura for what happened. She had always been able to see through Harry's guise. She had never felt comfortable around him either.

At the conclusion of the meal Clara helped clear the table and then she listened to the children tell about their Christmas.

Ned, Grandfather and Al did the chores early that night, including Laura's. When all were finished Ned took Clara home. Ned told her what had happened. Her heart went out to Laura and she made up her mind to help any way she could.

Chapter XIX

I worked hard and the warden trusted me. The guards never worried about me either, especially when I was working with the stock. I had plenty of chances to escape but did nothing to hurt my chances for an early parole.

I did not like to write letters and rarely did, although I longed for news from home. Laura and Mother were good to write. Often their letters calmed me down and helped me keep my goal in sight.

I was most restless at Christmas. That is when I thought the most about the children. I kept a record of their birthdays and tried to figure how tall each one was when a birthday came up.

As each spring came, I was anxious to get the prison crops planted and to care for the new stock.

Every time John Holden came to Salt Lake City he visited with me and always encouraged me to keep up the good work. For many hours we discussed the possibility of capturing Jesse Challis and how to go about it. Little was said about Butch

Cassidy, but stories of his escapades circulated through the prison. I liked Roy and always hoped the stories were not true. John knew how I felt.

The spring little Al turned eight years old, Grandpa Albert sent word to Laura that he had a job for little Al, helping at a sheep camp for the summer. Laura's first impulse was that the boy was too young, but Al wanted to do it. The job would allow him to earn money to help his mother and sisters.

Laura decided to talk to Father, showing him the letter.

"Don't you think Al is too young and small for such a thing?" she asked.

"I don't blame you for wanting to keep him home," Hyrum responded. "He's a good helper for you, but if he wants to try it and if your father thinks he can do it, maybe he should. He surely would feel like a man if her were earning money to help his family."

"He seems like such a little boy to go so far away from home alone," lamented Laura. "But I guess I'll let him try it."

The next wagon leaving for Marysvale took little Al on his greatest adventure. Within three days he was at the herd learning his future summer occupation. At first he was camp tender, then herder. He became the main breadwinner for the family in his father's absence.

The routine of country life continued for Laura and the children. She worked and waited.

Ned married Clara that summer and they built a home in town.

About a year later, John Holden escorted a new inmate to the Utah State Prison. All the prisoners were anxious to find out who the newcomer might be and to hear what news he brought in from the outside.

It was mealtime when I first saw the new inmate. I recognized him and grinned from ear to ear. Short of being set free, nothing could have made me happier. It was Jesse Challis. How good it was to see him there where he belonged. I just wished I could have been one of those who captured him.

Walking past Jesse with my dirty dishes, I asked, "How does it feel to be where you belong, smart boy?"

Jesse glared up at me and replied, "Not for long, big shot. Not for long. I was double crossed."

"Who would do that to an honest person like you?" I laughed.

"You better mind your own business," he growled.

Happily, I returned to the stables, wondering how they trapped him. Since entering the prison, I had never felt happier. Maybe there was some justice in this old world after all.

A little later I was called to one of the visitor's rooms. John Holden was waiting for me. I told him how good it had made me feel to see Jesse Challis behind bars. I asked him how he had done it.

"A lot of trickery," he said. "Even had a little trouble keeping him alive after I caught him. Seems some of the cattlemen just wanted to string him up."

I asked him to tell me how everything else was down home. I asked if he had seen Laura and the children. I said I hadn't been receiving many letters.

"If you would write once in a while you might receive more letters," he said. I told him I thought it might be easier for them to forget me, that they would miss me less, if I didn't write very often.

"It works the other way," he said. "When they don't hear form you they worry more than ever. If you don't want them to worry about you, you should write to Laura and ask for a divorce."

The thought stunned me. I looked at John, feeling pain in my heart.

"Do you think she would want that?" I asked. "I don't know whether I could stand that although it might be best for her."

"She's a pretty woman," he said. "Do you think she should spend her whole life waiting for you?"

If John hadn't been a married man and a trusted friend, I would have questioned his intentions. Besides, he was old enough to be Laura's father.

"Think about it, Wil," he said as he got up to leave. "Write home more often. They miss you and love you."

"Thanks, John," I said. "I'll think about what you said. And thanks for bringing in Challis where I can keep an eye on him."

I thought about what John had said for the next few days. Finally, I sat down one night and wrote a letter.

Dear Laura:

I hope you are all well. It is good to hear from you anytime you can write. I am proud of Al for getting a job and helping to take care of his mother and sisters. That is better than his father is doing.

I'm well and trying to accept my lot. I brought it on myself so I must live with it.

They are allowing me to continue working with the stock and do some farming, all of which is good.

John Holden and I had a good talk last week when he brought Jesse Challis to prison. It really does me good to know they finally caught up with that crook.

John caused me to look at myself more clearly. I suppose I have been selfish and not very reasonable at times and the more I think about it the more I can see that he is probably right.

You are a young woman and it isn't fair for you to be tied to a ghost. I realize I haven't been the kind of a husband, father and provider that I should have been. So to ease your burden, and to be fair to you and the children, I suggest you get a divorce if you want to. I won't contest it. I have no right to do that.

Please understand that I am not suggesting it because I don't love you but because you deserve better than you are getting and I want you to have some happiness in life. I have no idea when I will get out of here and it isn't fair to you to keep waiting.

Think about it and don't worry about me. I doubt if I am worth your tears.

Wil

A few months later I received Laura's reply.

Dear Wil,

I have been doing what you asked me to do. I have been thinking and thinking until I am thought out.

I have decided not to worry any more about whether or not I should divorce you. I do not want a divorce. There is no use worrying anymore about it unless you want to do it.

All our troubles have not been your fault. They have been partly mine and some were no fault of ours at all.

I love you and intend to wait. If you want it some other way you will have to take the initiative. If you want a divorce, I will not contest it either.

We are getting along all right. Al is working most of the time now, coming home for part of the school year. He seems so grown up and mature for such a young boy. He sends all his earnings to us. We appreciate it so much and love him for what he is doing.

The girls are growing and send their love.

I love you and am waiting. Please come home when you get out.

Always thinking of you,

Laura

Chapter XX

The next few months went by without anything to interfere with the daily prison routines.

News from home indicated the cattle rustling had come to a complete stop. The cattlemen were convinced that Challis was involved in most, if not all, of the rustling. If there had been others, the Challis arrest had frightened them away, at least temporarily.

Ned and Clara had a baby boy and bought the Bybe farm. They still lived in town where they could help Laura as well as Father and Mother. Fruit trees were maturing and producing all the fruit the people needed. Some of it was freighted away and sold in other towns. The other crops were doing well too. The greatest need was for more good water because crops needed to be irrigated.

A town water system was conceived and launched. The plan included a reservoir near the head of the canyon which would capture spring run-off water and make it available throughout the hot summer.

My life was about the same as it had been for a lifetime, it seemed—feed the stock, clean the stables, help milk the cows, fix and paint fences and buildings. Sometimes it was monotonous, but much better than walking back and forth in a cell.

The work I liked best was riding and training the horses. Pacer was my favorite and few people touched him besides me. Once in a while the warden would ride him around the farm checking the work and crops.

I found out later that the warden and members of the parole board had talked about paroling me, but had not reached a decision as to when that might be.

One evening at bed check a prisoner was discovered missing. The warden was quickly notified and the supervising guards called in. The escapee was Jesse Challis.

As plans were being discussed to pursue Challis, the warden asked which guard was the best tracker. I don't know why, but no dogs were available at the time.

No one answered. Finally one of them spoke up. "The best tracker in this prison is not one of the guards."

"Who?" asked the warden.

"Wil Halladay."

"How do you know that?"

"John Holden has a dozen stories where Halladay, as his deputy, tracked down rustlers, criminals or Indians after everyone else had lost the trail. Holden says Halladay could be the best tracker in the territory."

"But he's an inmate," the warden said.

"Yes, but a trusted one. We all know he's had ample opportunity to escape but never has."

"Should we take the chance?"

"I would," answered the guard.

"Go get him. Challis has a good start on us."

Ten minutes later I followed the guard into the warden's office. He got right to the point, asking me if I wanted to help catch Challis. I didn't need any time to consider my answer. I wanted to help, as much as I ever wanted to do anything in my life.

"Can you do it?" the warden asked.

"I think I can," I answered.

"Can I trust you?"

"If you knew how I have felt about Challis, and all the years I have plotted and figured to get that rustler behind bars you wouldn't ask that. Besides, if he gets away he'll go back to stealing my cattle. I'll get him."

"How many men do you want, and when do you want to start?"

"My guess is he headed up the canyon— probably still running. I'll take Pacer, and a lariat or two. That'll do it."

"No gun?"

"If I took a gun I'd probably kill the son-of-a-bitch."

As the stars began to fade, I was on the trail.

At first Jesse hadn't worried about his tracks. All he wanted to do was to get away. His trail was easy to follow. He jogged up the stream towards the mountains as I thought he would.

Pacer kept up a steady, easy gate during the early hours. When I noticed Challis' tracks were beginning to weave and slide, I became more cautious.

Morning was hot and I could tell that Challis was hurting from the hours of pushing himself so hard. Months in prison had made him soft. He was in no condition for an extended march.

Slowing the panting, sweating Pacer to a walk, I patted his neck and spoke soft, kind words to him. The horse responded to my touch and moved along smoothly. Both of us were alert to every sound.

Looking ahead, I saw Jesse's tracks slide into the stream bed. It was almost noon and I guessed he had about reached the end of his endurance.

I stopped Pacer and dismounted. There was a tingling feeling in the back of my neck. We both drank quietly from the stream. I stood up, tied Pacer to a small cottonwood tree, and took the ropes from the saddle. I patted Pacer on the neck and told him to be quiet. Silently, I slipped off my shoes and put on the soft moccasins I had brought.

I figured that after a deep drink from the stream, Challis would need to rest. Having been on the trail so long, there would be a good chance he was asleep.

I moved quietly, listening intently to every sound, watching for any sign of Challis, or any unusual movement. Step by step I crept forward. Then I heard it—the deep, uneven breathing of a sleeping man. It was almost a snore. I moved around a full low-branched bushy tree, and there lay Jesse, sound asleep, sweaty, dusty and flat on his back. I guessed his feet were hot and blistered, and too sore to walk on.

Carefully, I tied a slipknot around one boot and anchored it to the tree, not tight, but snug, knowing that when Jesse jumped, the rope would tighten up. I then moved above his head with a small loop in the lariat, quietly laying one edge of the loop below Challis' chin with the knot on the ground above his head.

"Jesse," I yelled as loud as I could, once the loop was in place. The outlaw sat up with a jerk, allowing the loop to settle around his neck. I yanked hard on the rope. The surprised Challis couldn't get to his feet because one leg was tied to the tree. Both hands went to the rope around his throat. He tried to loosen it but I kept it tight.

"You're choking me," he gasped between clenched teeth.

"I sure am," I said, "and I'm enjoying it."

"Let up," he begged.

"I'm in no hurry," I said.

"I'll kill you," he gurgled.

"I doubt that, but if you don't want me to kill you, then quit floundering around and open those big mule ears of yours and listen," I warned him. "I can pull on this rope until you turn black and blue."

The lack of oxygen gradually had a quieting effect on Jesse. His twisting and turning, and grabbing for the rope slowed down, then stopped altogether.

"Listen carefully or I'll hit you over the head with this club," I warned, edging down towards him with a nice piece of oak in one hand and the rope in the other. "Turn over on your stomach. Now put your hands behind your back. I'll let up a little on the rope but don't try anything."

I eased up on the rope, and moved to tie Jesse's hands.

"I don't care if you try something stupid or not," I explained. "I almost wish you would so I could have good reason to lay you out cold."

Jesse lay still while I tied his hands behind his back. Then I cut the rope from his foot and helped him sit up, at the same time loosening the rope around his neck a little more.

Finally Challis looked up and recognized me. "So it's you! How did you get out?" he growled.

"That's my secret," I said. "Now stand up and let's start back. Walking downhill should be easier." I helped Jesse to his feet.

He flinched with pain as he stood on his sore, tired feet. "I can't walk," he moaned.

"Then I'll drag you back," I said as I started leading him to where I had tied the horse.

"I thought we were on the same side of the law," he said.

"We have never been on the same side and you know it," I told him.

As I led him towards the horse, Jesse grimaced with every step. "I hope we both get to ride," he said when he saw the horse.

"Pacer," I explained, "has never been trained to ride double, and he doesn't like rustlers."

"You're as much a rustler as I am, and a murderer to boot," he growled.

"Then I guess one more killing won't matter," I said. "Your life is a very small price for the agony you have caused me and my family."

I told him I was going to get on my horse and head down the trail. I told him it was a long way back to the prison and the horse was anxious to be on his way.

"If you want to follow on your feet, that's fine," I explained. "If you don't feel like walking, then Pacer will be happy to drag you. It doesn't make a whole lot of difference to me as to which way you decide to travel. The warden wanted you back alive," I said, "but I really don't care if you are or not. It's up to you."

I got on the horse, looped the free end of the lariat around the saddle horn, then eased the horse into his pace gait. I let him maintain that pace all the way to the prison. Challis cursed the entire distance. He was too angry to give up and let me drag him.

It was after dark when we reached the prison walls. I yelled for someone to open the gate. When I led Challis inside the horse finally stopped. Jesse sank to the ground. I threw the rope to a guard.

"Take good care of this one," I said. "Don't need to worry about him trying another break tonight."

The warden seemed very pleased, but didn't say anything. Not only had I come back, but I had brought the prisoner with me—alive.

"You'd better take him to the doctor first," I said, as the guards began to drag Challis to his cell. "He probably has blisters on blisters, and a few rope burns on his neck."

I patted Pacer on the neck. The horse was wet and gaunt.

"If you don't mind I'll put Pacer away," I said. "He needs a good rubdown and some grain. He's earned it today." I started to lead the horse away.

"Just a minute, Wil," the warden said. "The guards will take care of the horse. I want you to come with me." I followed him toward his office.

As we entered the warden produced a sandwich and a drink of cool milk from the cooler. "Hungry?" he asked.

"Sure am," I said as I took the food.

"Thanks for the job you did today," he continued. "It won't hurt your chances for parole. Now get some rest. You've earned it." After finishing off the milk and food I headed for bed.

Chapter XXI

The next day I was called to the warden's office and asked to tell the complete story of the capture of Jesse Challis to the warden and the board. I told them everything and then returned to the barns.

About a week later I was summoned to the office again. I asked the guard at the door if he knew why I had been summoned. He didn't answer.

When I was ushered in I was greeted by the head of the board. He told me the warden had recommended me for pardon, and that the governor had approved it.

Without being invited to do it, I sat down. I was dazed wondering if I had heard right.

"Here's your pardon, Wil," the warden said. "It's signed and legal. You're a free man. Good luck. One of the guards will take you to the clothing room to fit you out with street clothes." He paused, then said he wished he could let me take Pacer, but he couldn't.

"You know, Warden," I said. "I would be glad to take him off your hands and then you wouldn't have to worry about him anymore."

After we got through talking about the horse the warden explained how the new railroad went all the way to Marysvale. He said a guard would take me to town where I could catch the train. I would be home in a few days.

I sat with my head down looking at the pardon. I couldn't believe my eyes, yet there it was. It had never occurred to me that I would get out after only four years. I was so thankful Laura hadn't divorced me.

"Remember, we are all pulling for you," the warden said. "Here is enough money for your train fare and lodgings. Good luck." He shook my hand. So did the president of the parole board.

I was still in shock as I followed a guard to the clothing room. I was a free man. It didn't seem real, but I had the signed pardon in my hand.

The next morning I hurried to the new railroad depot, eager for my first train ride. I was told I could travel clear to Marysvale in one day.

I stood and watched others buy their tickets so I followed suit and bought mine. I followed the other people out the back door to the train. It was big, black and noisy. Steam hissed and disappeared. The noise was painful to the ears but music to my heart. This big black beast was taking me home.

I climbed the steps into the passenger car. I settled myself by a window and waited, anxious to be on my way. Soon the train started and I began to relax and enjoy the ride.

During my journey south, my mind reflected over the years. So much had happened. Everyone and everything had changed, except my love for Laura and my family. I had never stopped loving Laura, not for a minute.

"She said she would wait," I said to myself as the train rocked along. It would be so good to see everyone again. I could hardly wait.

In prison I had learned a lot about farming and I was sure I could do a much better job with the crops. I hoped the cattle herds were doing well enough to where we could start selling some each year for cash money. Father had worked hard and deserved to start letting up a little. I would help him do that.

As we sped along I thought about Roy. Had he really turned to rustling and bank robbing? I continued to hope the stories I had heard were false. I felt sorry for his parents.

The train reached Marysvale just before dark. I walked through the new depot admiring the building with its bright lights and new benches, its loading platform and the big ticket window. Now it would be easy for us to ship cattle to market. Goods could be brought in cheaper and quicker. The train would be a boon to the whole area for both shipping and passengers.

When I knocked on the Bybe's door, Leah opened it.

"Oh, it's you," she said, quickly turning and walking away. It hadn't occurred to me that anyone might be unhappy to see me. As I thought about it I couldn't blame her. I had killed her husband.

"Who is it Leah?" her mother called from the other room.

"Him," Leah answered as she went up stairs to her room.

Mrs. Bybe came to the door.

"Wil," she exclaimed as she threw her arms around me, "have you been paroled?" She looked a little bewildered.

"No, better, I've been pardoned," I said. "Is Mr. Bybe home? I need to borrow a horse. I'd like to leave for home now."

"You should wait until morning," she said. "Come in and get something to eat. You can stay here tonight."

"I'd kinda like to be on my way."

She left and in a minute Mr. Bybe came into the room. He shook my hand, and congratulated me for getting an early out. He tried to get me to come into the living room and sit for a while, but I refused his invitation.

As I followed him to the barn, I gave him a short explanation of the events that led up to my release.

"I'm sure glad," he kept saying. "I think it's wonderful. Bring Laura and the children over to see us soon."

I saddled the horse and put some oats in one of the saddle bags. Mrs. Bybe came out and slipped something in the other bag.

"Thanks," I said as I mounted and rode south into the dark.

I walked the horse up the dugway leading out of town. As soon as we were on level ground I urged the horse into a trot. We kept that up till near midnight when I stopped at a small stream to give him a breather and let him drink. I fed him some grain from the saddle bag. He ate it hungrily. I discovered a sandwich in the other bag. Thanks to Mrs. Bybe's thoughtfulness I would not fast all the way.

The summer night was cool. I untied my coat from the back of the saddle and put it on. I decided to try the trail up the East Fork of the Sevier River. I had traveled that way once and figured it was shorter.

We trotted mile after mile. Twice more I stopped to rest the horse. Each time I gave it a drink and more of the oats. It was just getting light when I reached the top of the divide where the road led down to my home and loved ones and the little town that people now called Tropic. I slowed the horse's pace so he wouldn't suffer in the morning heat.

I couldn't help but think how different I felt this time. Last time I had been intent on getting even with Harry. How beautiful that little valley was. It wasn't green or large or narrow or anything in particular but it sure looked magnificent to me.

About 10 a.m. Laura Belle and Jolene ran into the house telling their mother a stranger was putting his horse in their corral.

"What does he look like?" Laura asked.

"He has a hat and a suit, and he is wearing a moustache."

"Not many men ride in a suit," she said as she started for the back door. When she opened it she saw me standing there, tired and dusty, but so glad to be home.

"Oh, Wil, Wil," she screamed as she threw her arms around my neck.

"Laura," I said as I grabbed her in the tightest bear hug she had ever received.

Nothing else was said for a few seconds as we stood there enjoying a postponed greeting. How we had both dreamed of this moment.

"Come in, you must have ridden all night," she said, after catching her breath. "Sit down while I get you something to eat. You must be starved."

"Oh, girls," she cried. "I almost forgot. This is your father. He's home to stay?" she said with a question in her voice as she looked at me.

"No, I didn't escape. I'm really through. I'm out. I'm home to stay," I said, turning to the girls.

Laura Belle acted as if she couldn't remember me at all. It hurt to have her look at me as a stranger, yet I realized it had been years since she last saw me.

In spite of myself I searched the face of Jolene for traces of Harry, but could find only sweet reminders of Laura. I realized that as long as Jolene was Laura's, she was my child, too.

"They were so young when you left, Wil," Laura said. "Give them time."

"Where's Al?" I asked.

"He's with the sheep, the dear boy. He has been such a help to us all." Laura showed me a place at the table and placed some eggs and potatoes before me. She said that when I finished eating she was going to put me to bed for a long nap. She winked at me in a way the girls didn't notice.

The food tasted so good, but I couldn't keep my eyes off the girls and Laura. I wondered if this could be what heaven was like. I wanted to know everything, about how everyone was and what had been happening. I asked about my mother and father.

"They are all right but the troubles have taken their toll," she said. "As soon as you finish eating we can walk over to see them, if you wish."

As we walked to my parent's home I told Laura about the events leading to my early release. It felt wonderful to walk and talk with her. The girls were still a little reluctant to talk to me.

Mother saw us coming and rushed out the front door. She stood there sobbing, holding me tightly in her arms, asking if I was home to stay.

"Yes, Mother, I'm home for good. Where are Father and the rest?"

"He and Ned rode up on the mountain to check the cattle this morning. Come in. I want to have a good look at you."

Just then Nancy and Ellen came running out the front door. They hadn't forgotten me. But they were so grown up and mature. I could hardly believe they were my little sisters.

What a joy it was to see them all so well after all the troubled years.

"Both of you have become beautiful women," I said.

"But still old maids," Nancy replied.

"I'll bet not for long," I said.

We talked till noon when Mother fixed a sandwich. I fell asleep in my chair while eating.

"Come on, Wil," Laura said. "Let's take you home and put you to bed where you belong."

"Not in the middle of the day," I protested. "Besides I want to talk to Father and Ned when they return. I want to see Blackie too."

"You'll see him when Ned returns," Laura said, pulling me out of my chair. "You can see old Pete too. The girls ride him once in a while."

"In fact," Laura said to the girls. "How would you like to stay with Grandmother this afternoon and ride Pete?" The girls squealed their delight.

"When were you released?" Mother asked, as Laura hurried me towards the door.

"Two days ago. I'll tell you all about it tonight when Dad and Ned get home." Laura and I hurried back to the cabin, eager to begin the rest of our lives.

Chapter XXII

The next morning early, one of the neighbors came over while I was doing chores. It was Claud Johnson. He walked to the corral gate while I was feeding the horses.

"Howdy Wil. Good to see you home."

"Hello, Claud. How are you?"

"Not so good. I need help."

"What's wrong?"

"You remember my son Reggie, don't you?"

"Sure, he used to do chores for me. He also helped me build some of my fences. How is he?"

"He and his girl friend had a quarrel last week. He came home very upset, changed clothes, saddled his horse and rode away. Haven't seen him since. I'm afraid something has happened. He has been gone five days now. I heard you were in town last night. You're the best tracker in these parts. Will you help us please?"

"How was he mounted?" I asked.

"His little bay mare. She has a new colt so I don't see how he could have gone very far."

"Did he take a gun?" I asked.

"It's missing, so I guess he did."

"After breakfast I'll saddle up and ride over to your place."

"I'll go with you," Claud said.

"Maybe you ought to stay with your wife. I'll take Ned with me."

"All right," Claud said. He turned and started walking home.

"You've hardly been home a day," Laura said when I told her I was leaving.

"I have a feeling I'll be back before sundown," I said.

"What about food and water?" Laura asked.

"Won't need anything but my canteen," I said. I had that tingling feeling on the back of my neck that told me it was going to be an ugly day, and I wouldn't be in the mood to eat.

Ned agreed to go along so we saddled the horses and rode over to Claud's.

"Show me the mare's tracks, if you can, and we'll start there," I said.

Claud took me into the corral and showed me the mare's hoof prints. She had shoes on the front feet, but none on the hind feet. He showed me the stall where Reggie usually fed the mare.

After examining the tracks in the stall, I walked out the gate and examined all tracks leading into the street. I found the mare's tracks. The colt was with her.

194

"I'll send Ned back if we need help," I said. "Either way, we'll see you tonight and plan from there."

I walked, leading Blackie, to the edge of town where the trail led south. I mounted, following the tracks carefully for about five miles.

I stopped. To the right of me were two sets of tracks leading off the trail. One showed shoes on the front feet and the other set belonged to a colt. I turned and started up along the ridge where the tracks led me. The trail was easy to follow.

After about two miles, the tracks suddenly turned left toward some cliffs. I saw a movement under a big juniper.

"I think we've reached the end of the trail," I said to Ned.

Ned followed me down the side of a hill and up to the big tree. In the shade lay the dead colt. The mare was still tied to the tree. She had chewed off all the limbs and bark she could reach.

Beyond the mare, under a small tree lay Reggie. It looked as if he had held the gun under his chin and pulled the trigger. It was a gruesome sight.

We untied the mare and poured what water we had in one of our hats and let her drink it.

I told Ned to ride back and get Father and some of the other men. I told him to bring a big sack and some canvas, also some grain and more water for the mare.

"I'll stay here and wait for you," I said. "There isn't anything to do for Reggie but wrap him tight in a sack and canvas. We'll have to handle the body carefully."

Ned left and I sat down in the shade of a tree, off to the side, to wait and watch and think how close I had been to the same fate. I remembered times in prison when I wished I could die. Fortunately a gun was not available to me.

As I sat there in the shade, I thought about all that had happened to me in recent years. I felt cheated in some ways and lucky in others. A chipmunk kept darting out to look at me, concerned I was invading his territory. In addition to scolding me, he was busy putting up food for the winter, much as people did. I guessed the chipmunk life was a simple one, though, not complicated like the human condition.

A flock of bluejays flew over, darting from tree to tree searching for food. When they landed in a tree they would jump from limb to limb looking for any food tidbit that might help them survive. All nature seemed to be moving in the same path, trying to find the things that would keep them happy and alive. The more I looked at Reggie's body the more I realized that we couldn't take him back on a saddle and there was no way we could get a wagon up in the hills this far. We would have to transport him on a travois. I looked up the ridge and located a stand of quaking aspen. Without the benefit of an axe I had to settle for some dry poles that would serve the purpose.

Mounting Blackie I rode up the ridge to the green trees. Among them were quite a few fallen poles in different stages of decay. I tossed a rope around three of the trees and dragged them down the hill. Blackie found them easy to pull, and the dragging broke off most of the unwanted limbs.

I dragged the poles just below Reggie's body before removing the rope from around the saddle horn.

I was glad to see the mare still standing. If she had laid down it would have worried me. She was trying to nibble on the brush close by, but was too weak to move far. I spoke to her and patted her neck.

I placed the two strongest poles about two feet apart and started to weave my lariat back and forth in a web fashion, so we could place some canvas or ropes on it to hold the body. With more ropes over the top, I figured we could hold it in place long enough to drag it to the road where we could lift the body into a wagon.

I hoped that Claud would not come with the rest of the men but I was almost sure he would. I didn't want him to see Reggie's body in that condition.

I was about finished weaving the rope when I heard Blackie nicker. I looked up at him and noticed that he was looking down the ridge. Ned was leading about a half dozen riders. One of them was leading a pack horse. Claud was with them.

Claud was the first one off his horse. I pointed toward Reggie's body. Claud walked over to the body and stopped. I knew his heart was breaking. I could see him grit his teeth. The muscles in his neck bulged as he looked at what was left of his son.

"Claud," I said, touching his arm. "Let us take care of his body while you see to the mare. I hope someone brought some water and feed."

"The pack bags are full of hay and we have a small keg of water," Claud said without taking his eyes from his son.

"Please, Claud, take care of the mare and let us handle this," I said again. Taking him by the hand I led him to the animal. He put his arms around her neck and buried his face in her mane. She gave a weak whinny and turned her head towards him.

Ned brought a sack of feed to the horse. She grabbed a mouthful but it seemed an effort for her to eat. When he produced a pan and poured some water in it she gulped it down quickly. After a little more water she began to eat the hay with more relish.

While Claud and Ned were working with the mare the other men helped me wrap Reggie's body in the canvas and sacks and tie it on the travois. One of the men said my father was waiting for us at the road with a wagon.

The next week, even before I had a chance to ride up on the mountain and look at the cattle, John Holden rode in.

"What are you doing down this way?" I asked after our greeting.

"Believe it or not I'm after you," he replied.

I looked at him questioningly.

"I don't mean I am after you that way. I need help again. Here, look, this is your old badge. I've been instructed to swear you in again if you will help me. Of course you'll get a raise in salary. Raise your right hand."

I stood looking at him. "Is this some kind of a joke?"

"No, it's no joke," he answered. "Raise your right hand."

"You're serious?"

"I don't know how many of them want you besides me and the governor. It doesn't matter. Now raise your right hand."

"Not so fast, not so fast," I protested. "Start from the beginning and tell me what this is all about."

"We have some trouble down south and I need help."

"What about old Charley. Can't you use him?"

"He won't go unless you go."

"You see, John, I had decided not to get mixed up in other people's business any more. I don't want to go with you."

"You brought Challis back," John reminded me.

"That was different."

"If we don't stop this new bunch they might be worse than Challis some day," John said.

"I haven't even seen my son, Al, yet."

"We'll be back in a few days, then you can stay home till the next flareup."

"I suppose Laura could use the extra money."

"When the outlaws hear all three of us are after them, they'll leave the country fast," John promised.

"Laura won't like it."

"Let me talk to her. She knows we need to drive the crooks out. We have to put a stop to the plundering of outlaws. This time I'm afraid it's your friend, Butch Cassidy."

"I don't believe it," I said in defense. "Roy wouldn't steal from people like us."

The next morning the pack mule was loaded and we were ready to head over to Charley's place. When I mounted Blackie, John asked where my guns were.

"I don't want them," I answered.

"Now look, Wil, there may be a half dozen or more. Do you think you can rope them all?"

"You and Charley can carry the guns."

"You're as stubborn as that pack mule," John said. He paused. "Will you go over to your father's place and get another rope then?"

While I was gone John went in the house and asked Laura for my six-shooter and carbine. He slipped them in my bed roll and was waiting when I returned with the extra rope.

Goodbyes were said with Laura pleading for me to hurry back.

"We will," John promised as he took the lead up the trail.

Word soon spread that John Holden, Charley Dutson and I were out to clean up the outlaw gangs roaming the area. Not wanting to confront us, the outlaws must have headed for less troublesome pastures. We never found any of them.

Life was getting more peaceful in our part of the West. Constant patrols by us kept the country around there a decent place to live and raise families.

We kept working our land and building homes and barns for new settlers. Town halls and churches began to spring up.

The next year a girl was born to us. We named her Mary Elizabeth after both of her grandmothers.

The cattle business was improving and the farms were producing good crops of every kind.

Bees were brought in to help pollinate the fruit trees and to produce honey. Watermelons and cantaloupes, along with every kind of berry that could be found, were brought in and planted. The area was conducive to growing nearly anything.

Laura was the best singer in the valley and she was constantly in demand. At last we were happy and content, with very little to worry about. Occasionally I was called upon to track down an outlaw and bring him in. I never liked to use a gun but I decided to carry one after that one trip with John. When it was time to make an arrest I usually left the rifle in the scabbard and used my rope.

Charley and John were getting older and liked the endurance rides after outlaws less and less. I began to do a lot of that kind of work by myself. Sometimes I took Ned, who worried me because of his lack of caution around dangerous types. Ned seemed to trust everyone.

One evening, near sundown, I pushed my shovel in the damp earth and walked to where Blackie was standing under the shed munching hay. I had been irrigating a hay field all day. Later one of us would have to ride up to the farm and change the water to another setting for the night. If we spread it out a little thinner it would be all right till early morning.

I mounted and rode down the canyon lane toward town, the evening chores and my night meal. When I neared home I saw extra animals in the corral and there under a young shade tree sat John Holden and Charley Dutson. I knew something important was up or those two wouldn't be there.

I hung the saddle up and put Blackie in the stable before I walked to the shade tree to greet the two men. "Hello, is this just a social call or are you two lost?" Neither responded. "I'll bet this coming trip must be exciting to get you two hermits out of your wickiups and away from your comfortable seats in the sun," I said.

"I doubt that you will consider it very exciting at all," John said.

I looked at him a little puzzled.

"The governor wants all three of us to go."

"I'm assuming you want to leave in the morning."

"Yes. Would you like to know where we are going?"

"I suppose that wouldn't hurt," I replied.

"Washington has been trying for months to set up a peace pow-wow with the Indians for this whole area from the Dakota's to the Grand Canyon. General Littlefield is heading up the Army delegation. The last word I got was that it would take place in the Ashley Valley near the Green River. The Mountain Men and the Indians used to rendezvous there nearly every summer."

"You want me to go with you to a pow-wow with the Indians?" I asked.

"Yes, the governor thinks it will give us a chance to get acquainted with the Indian agents, along with meeting many of the chiefs," John continued.

"I'll get things ready. How long will we be gone?"

"I imagine a week or two. Maybe three."

I went to tell Laura and to get my gear together. I sent word to Ned that I would be gone and for him to take over the watering. It didn't take long to get my gear together because I always had my pack in a more or less ready to go condition. Sometimes it was necessary for me to leave in a hurry. Usually we traveled light, securing camp meat on the way.

The constant strain of my leaving at a moment's notice, added to the risk that I might not ever return, kept Laura worried. I didn't blame her as she had been alone so much during our married life.

Chapter XXIII

A few days later we rode into one of the biggest encampments there had ever been in the Ashley Valley. Clusters of Indian tepees lined the stream for what seemed nearly a mile. The different tribes separated themselves from one another by camping in circles. Usually there was a larger lodge in the center of the circles. At one end of the camp there were rows of army tents.

John led the three of us to an army tent where a flagpole held an American flag waving in the breeze. He dismounted and reported. We were told to camp by the other lawmen near the army garrison.

Charley stayed close to John and me. He was not a full-blooded Indian; therefore some of his people rejected him. To us he was a good Indian, regardless of his breeding, because we could trust him. He was a good man to have on your side in a fight.

Our horses were hobbled near our tent. Guards were patrolling all army properties.

The next morning while John conferred with the army, Charley and I decided to take a walk among the Indian camps. I had always been eager to learn more about Indians ever since I had been rescued by Red Owl. As we walked along Charley pointed out various markings on the tepees, and explained their meanings.

After a while we came upon a circle of chiefs in earnest conversation. "What are they discussing?" I asked.

"I don't know all the different tongues," Charley said, "but I can read most of their signs and they are going over some of the problems they expect the general to bring up."

As we walked past the group and moved toward the next circle of tepees, I suddenly stopped. Someone behind me had spoken my name. One of the chiefs from the group we had just passed, was standing up, his hand raised high. "Wil," he shouted again.

At first I couldn't think who it might be, then suddenly I realized it had to be Red Owl. He was tall and stately and wore a heavy chief's headdress reaching almost to the ground.

"Red Owl?" I asked, still not totally sure it was him.

The tall Indian nodded that he was indeed Red Owl. He said something to the other chiefs in the circle, then started walking towards us. I hurried towards him. We grasped each other's arms in a strong grip.

"Me glad to see you, Wil," Red Owl said. "You here to help make peace?"

"Yes," I said. He smiled.

I introduced him to Charley. I told him we worked together when there was trouble.

"He my friend too," Red Owl said, then he asked where I lived and what I was doing for a living.

I told him, then asked him if he had become a chief?

"Yes, me chief," he answered.

"What tribe do you belong to?"

"Omaha," he said.

"I hear your people have helped keep peace for many years."

"We don't need more fighting. Red man and white man should be friends," he said.

"If only the white men could be fair," I said. He nodded his agreement.

"You come with me and tell generals that," he said. "Your words help our people."

"I'd be glad to tell the government men about how I feel, but you see I cannot make decisions for my government. I'm sure they wouldn't even let me in to the meetings, and they certainly won't let me give my opinion."

I told him about my family, and thanked him for saving my life. I invited him to visit my place in Tropic, and he invited me to his reservation.

We shook hands, both promising to see each other more during the week. He returned to the circle of chiefs. I knew our paths would soon part, perhaps never to cross again, yet the friendship between us was strong. It was good to see him again.

The trip was a profitable one for all concerned. We met many of the leaders of the Indian tribes and many of the law enforcement personnel. A good peace plan was approved.

On the evening of the fifth day the conference ended. The next morning, by the time the sun appeared over the mountains, John, Charley and I were in our saddles heading west.

Little was said during the day as we traveled towards our homes. John felt sure that the rendezvous had achieved its goals.

That evening we found a secluded spot next to a ledge near a small stream of water where the grass was tall and plentiful. It was a beautiful place and secure from wandering eyes. Precaution was still part of our way of life when on the trail.

"I think I should report to the Governor as soon as I can," John said that evening. "I'll leave you two in the morning and head for Salt Lake City."

"Don't worry about us," I told him. "Charley and I want to turn south anyway. We want to try to find Roy and talk to him. I don't believe all the stories about him, and neither does Charley."

"Maybe Butch has changed since you two knew him," John offered.

"I worked with him, drank with him, lived with him. He was the best man at my wedding. I think I know him. I don't think he could have changed that much, and I know he is not as bad as they say he is."

"I hope you're right," John said. "Good luck and be careful."

"Where do you think we ought to look for him, Browns Hole or the Roost?"

John thought for a minute before he answered. "I think I'd try the Roost. Brown's Hole is too close, with all the lawmen and Army in the area for the pow-wow. The Roost is a lot further away, and safer. I'll bet he's there."

"How would you get there?" I asked.

"Once you get to Green River, go south by southeast, about 30 or 40 miles. If you get to Hanksville you've gone too far. It's about 20 miles northeast of Hanksville, on the edge of the swell. It has a good spring and cattle for miles around head in there to drink. You'll see the trails. Lots of good spots where you can get ambushed."

I think he was trying to discourage us, but we said nothing. We would have to think about it overnight. I really wanted to find Roy and find out what I could. John said he knew of only one law man who had ever made it in and out of Robbers

Roost. He rode in on a horse and came out on foot, no boots and no pants either.

The next morning we parted. Charley and I headed south while John started toward Salt Lake with his report.

I wasn't a talkative man and Charley never wasted words at any time. We rode for miles, up canyons and over mesas, through sagebrush flats, around trees and rocks, especially rocks. We talked little and were always on the alert for danger. On the second day out of Green River we located a faint trail that we thought might lead us to the Roost.

Charley said he hadn't been in the country before because there was little game there. With nothing to hunt, there was little reason for Indians to go there. He said, however, from what he had heard, the country was not as rough as many of the white men thought.

We were seeing an increasing number of cattle tracks, but no buffalo or deer sign.

It looked like pretty good cattle country to me, with both summer and winter range. The rancher that ran his cattle here would not have to put up hay.

Towards the end of the day we left the trail and followed a side canyon until we found a small spring. We made camp for the night.

Early the next morning we returned to the flats and found the trail again. We followed it down a small canyon. From the ledges on both sides of us I began to understand why lawmen were hesitant to come here. There were plenty of places to ambush someone you didn't want in the area.

Just then a man with a rifle in his hands stood up on one of the ledges. Charley and I stopped.

"Who are you and what do you want?" the man asked.

"We're looking for Roy Parker, an old friend," I shouted.

"Are the two of you alone?" the guard asked.

"Yes," I answered.

The guard paused a minute before he went on. "Ride on down to the cabin. Ask someone there. Just follow the trail, but don't try anything stupid. You're being watched all the time."

I figured we could be in big trouble if Roy wasn't around to speak up for us. Perhaps we were stupid trying to find him.

"What do you think?" I asked Charley. "Should we turn back? This could get dangerous."

"I say let's keep going," he said.

I felt the badge in my pocket and pushed it further down toward the bottom. I told Charley to do the same. I didn't want anyone to know we were anything but Roy's friends. If he were there then it didn't matter.

We rode carefully down the canyon, spotting other guards along the way. The mouth of the canyon opened into a small valley. By a ledge was a beautiful spring not far from a shallow cave. On the other side of the water stood an old sun-bleached log cabin. A corral had been built close by encompassing part of the stream.

Men were standing in different places watching us as we stopped at the spring to water our horses and ourselves. After I quenched my thirst I stood up and turned toward the cabin. There stood Roy, just in front of the door.

"Hello, cowboys," he said. "What in the world are you two doing here?"

A flood of memories flashed through my mind as I looked at Roy. He looked good, but older and more mature. His shoulders were broad and his face tanned. He stood straight and tall. He still had the same big smile, and the twinkle in his eye had not dimmed. He had a full moustache. When we were in the mines he had tried two or three times to grow one but it never seemed to grow like he wanted it to. Now it looked healthy and permanent. How I had missed Roy and his happy disposition. Now here we were in one of the most desolate places I had ever seen, apparently on different sides of the law. But I decided that no matter what he had done, I would always like him.

"We're looking for you," I said, watching him carefully.

"Looking for me?" he asked, the grin remaining. "What for?"

I didn't answer so he continued. "Surely you haven't come to take me in, have you?" he asked. "I heard both of you are state officers."

Charley and I walked up to him. "Is there any reason why I should take you in?" I asked.

"I suppose there might be if you believe all the stories you hear," he said, reaching out his hand. "It's good to see both of you."

"We've not come on official business," I said as I shook his hand. "We were in the area and just thought we would drop in and visit an old friend."

I told him I'd heard a lot of stories about him. I wanted to know if there was any truth to the stories, or if he had a twin brother.

"I have no twin brother so there must be a ghost or two that looks like me," he grinned.

"I wish it were so," I said as I looked at some of his friends nearby.

"What have you heard, Wil?"

"That you've been stealing stock, and robbing banks and trains all over the West."

"Don't believe all you hear, Wil," he said. "We've been having a little fun but you know how people exaggerate."

"I know something else, too," I said. "You sure have a lot of friends around the country. Most of the folks I know hope you don't get caught, and they won't help the law find you."

Roy smiled and looked away for a few seconds. "I hope you two are still my friends. We had good times together in the mines."

"Yes, we're still your friends," I said. "We haven't forgotten the good times. Hope we never have to come after you."

"Don't worry," he said. "There's nothing in the southern part of the Utah Territory that I want. But tell me, when did you get out of the big house?"

"Not very long ago. That's no place to be, not even for you."

Roy motioned for us to sit down in the shade by the cabin. We talked about my experiences in prison. I told him about the rendezvous and how I had finally found Red Owl. Roy remembered the story I had told him about Red Owl saving my life.

When we got up to leave I asked Roy if he had ever thought about marrying and settling down.

"I've often thought about that, Wil," he said. "Father came to see me a few times to get me to come back home. But if I do that, they'll lock me up on suspicion of all the crimes I'm supposed to have committed. I just don't know how I can go back. And I could never marry a woman and bring her into this kind of life."

We stood there without speaking for a few seconds. I realized Roy felt like I did when I was in prison. He wasn't free to live a normal life. He was a slave to the outlaw trail.

"Yes, I think I can understand," I said.

I looked around, finally realizing that much of what I had heard about Roy was true. He was still the same, friendly Roy I knew in Marysvale, but he was also an outlaw, and a damn good one if only a fourth of the stories were true. My friend Robert LeRoy Parker was indeed the notorious Butch Cassidy.

The sun was high and hot in the clear blue sky. It was a peaceful spot, but a lonely place too, a good place for men on the run.

"Well," I said as I turned to Roy. "I think I have the answers I came looking for. Maybe we'd better be on our way. I wish you would come home with us, but I don't blame you for not wanting to take the chance on going to jail. I know I don't ever want to be locked up again. Good luck and goodbye, Roy."

We shook hands again. Roy said he would have one of the boys show us the trail out.

Roy followed me to my horse. He held on to Blackie's mane as I put my foot in the stirrup and swung my right leg over the saddle.

"Do you recognize him, Roy?" I asked. He looked at me, puzzled.

"The horse, Roy," I said. "Surely you remember. This is the one you gave me for a wedding present."

"No bull," Roy said as he looked closer at Blackie. He walked all the way around the horse. "Looks good." Suddenly his face changed and his eyes drifted off to the top of the sand cliffs above the little canyon. "I'd love to hear Laura sing again," he said. How is she anyway?"

"She'll sing for you anytime," I said. "Come and see us."

"Wish I could, Wil," he said. "Wish I could change my name back to Roy, and forget everything that's happened since Marysvale. But I guess it's just too late."

"What happened, Roy?" I asked.

"We started betting on horse races and playing poker. We were having a lot of fun but it just snowballed. I didn't intend for things to go this far."

We shook hands again, our eyes meeting for just a moment. Finally, I turned, mounted Blackie and started up the trail, following our guide. When we reached a twist in the trail where it disappeared behind a small sandhill, I turned and looked back. Roy was still standing by the cabin, watching us. I wondered what would to happen to him.

I still thought he was one of the finest people I ever met. Instinctively I knew he would not turn himself in and face going to prison. He would probably die doing pretty much what he was doing now.

Chapter XXIV

Finally, Laura and I had another boy. We named our second son, Ray. We didn't know at the time he was to be our last child.

When Ray was about a year old, Elizabeth sent word to Laura that Albert had to go to Salt Lake City on a business trip and they would like Laura to go along with them. Leah had gone on the last trip, so now it was Laura's turn. They were sure she would enjoy it. She would be good company for her mother while Albert was handling his business.

Laura was eager to go, but I was worried and I didn't know why. After all the times I had left her to worry while I was off chasing criminals, there was little I could say when she wanted to go to Salt Lake City with her parents.

It was agreed that our oldest daughter, Laura Belle, would stay home and take care of things there while Jolene went to Marysvale to stay with Leah to help care for the small children. Al volunteered to drive them all to Marysvale, then come home until it was time for them to return.

Even though Al was a small lad, I knew he was very responsible and could handle it with the help of friends along the way.

The morning for the departure came. After farewells were said, they got into the buggy to leave. Laura began to cry and I felt like doing it too.

"Be careful and don't get hurt," I cautioned, vaguely remembering that Laura usually said something like that to me every time I left home.

"We will," Laura promised as she kissed me again and waved goodbye to the others. "Laura Belle, now be careful and take good care of my menfolks."

Laura always shed tears when we parted. She looked back and continued to wave as they drove towards the canyon.

When the roads were dry one could travel to Marysvale in a day and a half, so the next day about noon the team trotted around the curve and down the hill into town.

Al walked to the depot that evening to see the train come in. It was a glorious sight for the boy. He hoped that someday he could go for a ride on it. He was happy for his mother and thankful that his grandparents would take her along. Life hadn't been easy for her and he knew she deserved a vacation of some sort. He looked forward to picking her up on her return.

The next morning he left for home about the same time the train left. When he got to the top of the dugway, he stopped and watched the train pull out.

Laura was very excited. She had never been to the big city before and had never ridden on a train. She held onto the seat as the engine puffed black smoke, blew its whistle and jerked forward as the brakes were released and the steam shot out each side.

Her mother relaxed and sat back in the padded seat. "Don't worry dear, it's only noise."

Down the canyon they went, around each bend and across the river, rocking back and forth while watching the changing landscape. Soon they were flying through open valleys, speeding past farms and pastures. Cattle and horses on both sides pricked up their ears and watched the smoking monster roll by.

Before dark that evening they reached Salt Lake City. They went to the Hotel Utah where Albert had reserved a room. It was so beautiful that Laura was almost speechless. She gazed around in awe.

"Oh, Mother," she said. "Wouldn't it be heaven to live here all the time?"

"There are some lovely places and sights here, but home is home," Elizabeth replied.

Laura had a hard time sleeping that night. The sounds of trains, street cars and people were so different from the sleepy little village of Tropic.

For two days Elizabeth led Laura from place to place. The stores were filled with hundreds of things she'd never seen before.

"It's so exciting," Laura exclaimed. "I wish I could stay a long time."

The afternoon of the third day Albert was free, so they rode a streetcar to Liberty Park to meet some friends for a picnic. Big grassy lawns with cages of small animals and birds were on display. There was a bandstand on one side where a brass band played.

Meeting them at the park, standing under a big tree, were Jake and Lottie Atkens. Jake had been an attorney for one of the other mining companies until they closed the mine. Then he had moved to Salt Lake City to continue his practice. Jake and Albert had maintained their close friendship over the years. Jake carried a picnic basket filled with plenty of home cooked food.

Laura absorbed the atmosphere of the park, wishing her family could be with her. She thanked her Father in Heaven for making it possible for her to come on such a wonderful journey. She knew she would never forget it.

They were scheduled to catch the train for home the next morning so they left the park early. They wanted to pack their things back at the hotel before dark. Laura wanted to ride the streetcar to the hotel—one more thing she had never done before coming to the big city.

The sun had set when they reached the hotel. Albert stepped down first, then turned to help Elizabeth. Laura followed her mother, but as she began to step to the ground, the streetcar jerked. Laura lost her balance and fell to the street, striking her head.

Laura didn't move.

"Laura, are you hurt?" Albert and Elizabeth asked, again and again with no answer.

People from all directions came to help. They wanted to know if she was all right.

A policeman hurried over and asked the crowd to move back and give her room. When he saw she wasn't moving, he sent someone for a doctor.

Kneeling beside Laura, the doctor noticed the back of her head was bleeding and quickly produced some bandages to place under her head. A wrap was rolled around the bandage and head to help stop the bleeding.

"How serious is it, Doctor?" Albert asked. "She's my daughter."

"I don't know yet," the doctor said.

"We're staying at the hotel," Albert volunteered.

"Then let's get some help" the doctor said, "and move her into her room."

Laura was laid on the bed. The doctor checked her blood pressure and heart and examined her eyes. He said she had a concussion and possible fractured skull and could be unconscious for a long time. He continued to examine her head.

When the doctor finally finished, he introduced himself as Dr. Blake. He said he wanted to call in another doctor. He wrote a note and handed it to a bellboy.

About half an hour later a second doctor appeared at the door. He introduced himself as Dr. Reid. Dr. Blake escorted him to Laura. When the two of them were finished examining Laura they both left the room for a few minutes. Dr. Blake returned and Albert looked at him for some hope or encouragement.

"Dr. Reid agrees with my diagnosis," Dr. Blake said. "She has a very bad concussion. We think her skull is fractured from the base to the crown."

"How serious is it?"

"You should know the truth. It is extremely critical."

Elizabeth began to cry, for the first time.

"Can you stay for awhile?" Albert asked. Dr. Blake nodded.

Albert paced the floor by Laura's bed. Elizabeth sat on the edge of the bed, crying and holding Laura's hand. She begged Laura to wake up and speak to her.

The dark night passed slowly. At about 3 a.m. Laura started to stir. She moaned and moved her hand. Elizabeth called for the doctor.

Dr. Blake walked over to the bed and checked Laura's pulse, hoping she might finally be gaining consciousness.

Laura moved again, and mumbled something.

"Laura, dear. This is your mother. Talk to me."

"Mother?" Laura moaned.

"Yes. This is Mother. How can I help you?"

"Mother."

"I'm right here."

Laura mumbled something, then became still. At 3:15 a.m. she died, having never regained consciousness.

"Oh, Albert, I just can't believe it," Elizabeth cried. "She was so thrilled and happy. Why did this have to happen?"

Albert put his arms around his wife and cried with her.

Dr. Blake pulled the sheet over Laura's face. "I'm sorry we couldn't do more."

The next morning before getting on the train, Albert sent a telegram ahead, informing Leah of Laura's death. He told her to send word to Wil.

Finally someone announced that it was time to board the train for Marysvale so they shook hands with their friends and shed more tears. Soon the Bybes were on their way home. Their daughter's body would follow later.

Chapter XXV

Leah had just awakened when the telegram arrived.

"It can't be true," she sobbed. When she read the last line she ran up the street to her friend Harold Rowley. By the time she found him she was crying so hard she could not express herself. She just handed him the telegram.

"This is terrible," he said. "How can I help?"

"Deliver this message to Wil," she cried.

"Sure, I'm on my way."

"Take any of Father's horses," she said.

Harold shoved the telegram in his shirt and ran to the Bybe barn. He saddled a big bay. Without another word he began his journey to Tropic.

The horse settled into a swinging trot and covered mile after mile in excellent time. Harold stopped two or three times to let the horse rest and drink.

I had been out on an assignment with Charley, and was hurrying home the same day that Harold was riding to Tropic. I was pushing Blackie pretty hard so I would be there when Laura arrived. I knew she would be excited about her trip and have many things to tell us. We had been separated so much, I didn't want us to be apart any more than was absolutely necessary. We were happy now and I planned to have it stay that way for the rest of our lives.

It was after midnight when the big bay arrived at my gate. Harold went inside and showed the telegram to Al. I wasn't home yet.

I arrived a little while later. I recognized the big bay tied to the front gate as one of Mr. Bybe's, I thought for a minute it might be Laura, thinking she had hurried home to be with me, not wanting to wait for the buggy ride.

When I stepped through the door and saw it was Harold, and not Laura, I was stabbed by a feeling of fear. The hair on the back of my neck stood up. I knew something was wrong.

"Mr. Rowley brought a telegram," Al said.

With hesitation, my hand beginning to shake, I took the envelope from Al. I turned towards the lamp. I started reading the message out loud but my eyes quickly scanned the page. I sank into a chair, my hands forgetting about the telegram as it fluttered to the floor.

Al picked it up and finished reading it. Laura Belle heard enough from the other room to know what had happened. She started to cry. Al turned and left the room without uttering another sound.

He closed the door and dropped on his bed, covering his head with his pillow.

I turned to Harold. "Thanks for bringing us the telegram. You must be tired and hungry if you have ridden all day and half the night." He sat down.

I walked to the bedroom door and asked Laura Belle to come out and fix Harold something to eat. I asked Al to go outside and take care of his horse—mine too. I was sure Al was glad to get out of the house and have something to do.

I looked at the telegram again. I looked at the date and realized the body would be arriving in Marysvale the next night. I realized that if we left right away we could be there when she arrived.

I told the children to hurry and get ready to go to Marysvale. I told Harold that after he had something to eat he could crawl in Al's bed and get some sleep. I thanked him again for bringing the telegram.

We harnessed the horses and hitched them to the light wagon. We tied a third horse to the back of the wagon, so we could rotate horses, and thus make better time.

While Al was catching the third horse, I grabbed a couple of quilts and threw them in the wagon box in the event one of us wanted to rest during the long journey.

We were soon in the wagon and heading out the gate. We stopped at Father's to let them know what had happened.

I walked in the front door and lit a lamp. My parents heard me and came into the room. I handed them the telegram, knowing I couldn't read it to them.

Mother began to cry. She asked if I had any more details about what had happened.

"Only that," I said pointing to the telegram. I asked Father to make sure the grave was dug close by. Then I turned and headed out the door.

We started up the road toward the top of the dugway. I didn't say much, fearing my emotions were too near the surface. I just kept driving, even though the horses didn't need that much attention. They knew enough to follow the road.

I was trying to make myself realize and accept the fact that my Laura was gone. We had been apart much of our lives but I always knew that when I went home, she would be there waiting for me. Now everything seemed so empty and final. My heart ached. I kept hoping I was having a bad dream, but knew I wasn't.

Laura Belle must have been reading my mind. She took hold of my arm. She said it was not a bad dream. Then she began to sob.

I put my arm around her, and tried to comfort her. In my misery I had not even thought of how she and Al might be feeling. I realized their hearts must be breaking, too.

All of my grief had been theirs also. A lot of it had been my fault and none of it theirs. We continued up the road, no one saying anything.

After reaching the top of the canyon it was downhill the rest of the way. Rotating horses helped us move faster and we reached Marysvale just after dark.

It was a sorrowful meeting. Elizabeth seemed to be taking it the hardest. She kept blaming herself for taking Laura with her to Salt Lake City. I told her about the feelings of anxiety I had before Laura left, and how I had done nothing to stop Laura.

When Leah walked in I could see that she had been crying too. She looked at me and saw the pain in my tired eyes. I wondered if I should leave. I felt sorry for her. She had lost her husband, and now her only sister. I was to blame for much of her pain. I turned to leave.

"Wil," she said, walking over to me. I stopped. She put her arms around me and we shed tears together. Wiping her eyes, she looked up at me.

"I'm so sorry for all the anger and hatred I have harbored all these years," she sobbed. "I loved my sister and I know how much you loved her. Please, forgive me."

"I forgive you and I hope you can forgive me," I replied. "I'm so sorry I caused you so much heartache and tears."

"I forgive you too and hope we can be friends again."

"Thank you, thank you."

As we stood there together with aching hearts, a great burden seemed to lift from my shoulders. I marveled at how much our lives had changed since we first met at that Saturday night dance.

Mr. Bybe came in the back door. He said the casket had just arrived on the train. He looked tired and drained. I asked him to tell me about the accident.

He sat down and told the whole story. "She was having such a wonderful time," he concluded.

"I'm glad of that," I said. "I haven't done much to make life pleasant for her. I wish I could have another chance."

"She loved you, Wil."

"I know. She spent most of our married life waiting for me," I stammered.

"And she's still waiting for you, Wil."

We sat in silence while I held my head in my hands.

"Shall we bury her here, or do you want to take her home?" Mr. Bybe asked.

"I want to take her home so I can be near her," I said. "My father should have the grave all ready when we get there."

There wasn't much sleep that night, especially for me. I think I relived every moment of our married life all over again, both the happy moments and the sad ones.

I had been happy in my early life even though we were poor. That never bothered me as I wandered through the woods hunting and fishing. Coming west was an exciting adventure for me, but when I met my Laura, everything seemed trivial compared to her. Now she was gone.

My heart ached as my tears rolled down my face onto my pillow. I wondered why something like this would happen. I didn't have any answers.

By early morning I had the casket in the wagon. Al and Jolene were with me as we headed for home. Mr. Bybe left a little later in his white-topped buggy with Elizabeth, Mary Elizabeth, Leah, her daughter Harriet, Laura Belle and baby Ray.

The next afternoon we drove into the new cemetery where the townspeople waited. The grave was ready.

After a song and a prayer, the bishop gave a short, glowing account of Laura's life. Slowly, her casket was lowered into the grave. The sun was going down. I turned and started walking toward the team and wagon with Laura Belle and Jolene holding onto my hands. Looking at them, I knew I must carry on even though my life seemed to be ending as the last rays of sunshine were fading from view.

One night about two weeks later, while I was lying in bed looking up at the dark ceiling, I heard a faint knock on my back door. I knew it had to be after midnight. Wondering who it could be, I put on my trousers, lit the oil lamp and walked quietly to the door.

Holding the lamp to one side, I opened the door and looked out. A man with a moustache and beard was standing there. His hat was drawn down low on his forehead. At first I didn't recognize him, but when his eyes flashed in the light, I realized it was Roy.

"Wil," he said in a low voice. "It's me, Roy. Step out here where we can talk without being heard."

I turned around and set the lamp on the table, then grabbed my coat which was hanging by the door. I blew out the light, then stepped outside. I grabbed Roy's outstretched hand.

"What in the world brings you to Tropic?" I asked. "Are you alone?"

"Yes, I'm alone," he said. "When I heard of Laura's death, I had to come and talk to you. You know how much I have always cared for you two. When I heard she had died I felt as bad as if it had been one of my little sisters. What happened, Wil?"

We sat down on a bench by the water pump and I told him the whole story. It was all I could do to tell him about the fall from the street car and bringing her body from Marysvale and the funeral. He took hold of my arm to comfort me.

We sat still for a few minutes, neither of us speaking. Finally he asked, "What are you going to do?"

"I have to carry on, keep the children together. That's all I have now."

"I'm so sorry, Wil. I wish it had been me instead of her. She had much to live for."

Nothing more was said for a little while. Finally Roy stood up. "I think I'd better go, but if you think I can help some way, please send word to me?"

"Thanks, Roy, but I think we'll be all right. My oldest daughter, Laura Belle, is helping a lot, and so are the others. I think we can manage."

Then I added, "Why don't you go home, Roy. Your parents would like to see you. They would like you to stay."

"You know I can't do that right now. Maybe some day, I hope." He held out his hand. "You take good care of yourself and those children. Maybe I'll drop in again sometime. Don't forget me. I'll never forget you and Laura." He pulled me closer to him. I wondered if he was going to put his arm around me but he didn't.

Without another word he turned and disappeared into the faint moonlight. I waited until I heard his horse head up the lane toward the breaks. I guessed he probably had a camp somewhere in those rugged canyons. I hoped he would visit his family before returning to the outlaw trail.

232

As I stood there listening to the sounds of vanishing hoofbeats, I shoved my hands down into my jacket pockets. I felt foreign objects in the right pocket. They were smooth and round. I pulled out, one by one, four double eagle gold pieces. I half choked as I thought about his thoughtfulness.

I couldn't help but chuckle. I was a deputy marshal, and my best friend was an outlaw. I prayed that I would never be asked to go after him.

The months dragged along. Sometimes I wondered if I would ever see Roy again. I heard many more stories about him and assumed some of them must be true. I worried about him and the life that he had chosen. At least he had all the excitement and danger he had ever wanted. All I could do was to hope and pray that he would change his lifestyle before it was too late.

I tried to return to a normal life but the numbness and shock of Laura's death was slow to leave. As it did, loneliness set in. It was worst when I returned home from trips. Laura wasn't there anymore, and I couldn't seem to get used to that.

I did all I could with the children, but thanked the Lord every day for Mother and my two sisters.

Sometimes I would saddle Blackie and ride up the lane towards the farm. After checking the crops I would continue up the trail toward those beautiful canyons and ledges where Laura and I had spent so many happy hours. We had often called the place our secret rendezvous. Eventually I would end up in the little canyon where we had that first picnic. The green grass still grew along the small stream that bubbled out of the ledge. The water was clear and cool and only ran a short distance before it sank into the dry earth. This had been our favorite place.

I would sit by the stream in the shade of those high ledges, close my eyes and think of Laura. Sometimes I could almost feel her sitting next to me. Sometimes I would open my eyes and look up at our initials carved into the north stone wall. Laura had scratched them there the first time we had come to this beautiful and now holy spot.

When we came back, she sometimes would take the time to dig the letters deeper into the rock. While she was alive I had never paid much attention to the initials, but now they were a link between us that was very precious to me. As I sat there it seemed she was near, so near, that when I looked up at the initials, I thought I could see her working on them to make them deeper. Then she would turn and look at me with that beautiful sparkle in her eyes.

I usually didn't stay long, but I did return often. This place was my own temple, my sacred place created by God and sanctified by Laura—the only place on earth where I could always feel Laura's spirit smiling down on me. It was here that my loneliness would be soothed just enough that I seemed to get my bearings for another little sojourn into life. Here all the shadows seemed to go the right direction and extend to the right places and I knew that it would be these long shadows that would someday lift me into Laura's arms.

About the Artist

Cover Artist, "Painter of the West..." Greg Sievers, resides with his family in a two-story farmhouse in Idaho. The roots of his paintings surround him in the straw fields and gray skies of a Jefferson County countryside and the nostalgic tones of its pioneer history. Respect for diligence, risk-taking, hard work and solemn responsibility weigh on the shoulders of his characters as they split wood, hoe weeds, churn butter under the watchful eye of Mother Nature.

Sievers has pulled from the local history he grew up with and the inspiration of some forefathers of art culture like Thomas Hill, N.C. Wyeth and Thomas Moran to create his own slant on the theme of Western life.

His slant isn't the shoot-em-up cowboys and Indians, as he puts it, but more the soul of Western cultures as it pits people against nature in a romantic battle of endurance that reflects his own admiration of the early tenants of this land.

This country has been the source of his inspiration and his determination to pursue the

Western theme. Sievers paints on location as much as possible and questions the inspiration of artists who paint exclusively from photographs. "Nature—that's where the real school is. I learn what the trees do, what the sun does." Art involves both inspiration and mechanics. Sievers senses a maturation of his work from his college days in Utah. "I'm beginning to convey a mood—I'm getting beyond just showing what I see. I'm showing what I feel. It takes maturity to go beyond what's obvious to what's meaningful."

He says that art has to speak on different levels to qualify as good art. He knows his paintings are going to mean different things to different people.

The course of Sievers' success as an artist is his willingness to work at it, he says, "I've seen good artists go by the wayside because they just weren't determined enough. It takes more than talent, it takes determination." Sievers' work is handled by major Western art galleries throughout the United States and Canada. He holds a BFA from Brigham Young University and an MFA from Utah State University.

Gregory Sievers, Painter of the West...
Route 1, box 35
Rigby, ID 83442